SORRY NOW?

SORRY NOW? • BY MARK RICHARD

ZUBRO · ST. MARTIN'S PRESS   NEW YORK

DESIGN BY JUDITH A. STAGNITTO

Library of Congress Cataloging-in-Publication Data

Zubro, Mark Richard.
    Sorry now? / Mark Richard Zubro.
        p. cm.
    ISBN 0-312-06470-5
    I. Title.
PS3576.U225S67   1991
813'.54—dc20   91-3098
                                                                           CIP

First Edition: September 1991
10 9 8 7 6 5 4 3 2 1

For my parents

ACKNOWLEDGMENTS

For their kind assistance, I wish to thank Bill Brill, Gerald A. Hannion, Jr., Alan Principe, Joe Valentine, and Paul Varnell

For their time, patience, and caring: Mike Kushner, Ric Paul, Kathy-Pakieser-Reed, and Peg Panzer

I wish to especially thank the Chicago Police Department and its men and women for their help in so many aspects of the book.

O N E

Paul Turner padded downstairs to his son Jeff's bedroom. Sunlight and birdcalls streamed in through the open window. The gauze curtains brushed against his hips as he stepped over his son's crutches. He paused, as he always did for a brief moment, to watch his son sleep. He noted the rise and fall of the thin chest, let his eyes rove over the shaggy hair. Neither Jeff nor his brother, Brian, believed in haircuts. Even shampooing their hair when they were little had been a major battle. He checked the leg braces on the floor and then ran his eyes over the catheterization equipment on the nightstand. Everything in place. Jeff stirred and turned on his stomach, the covers slipping down to reveal the years-old scar on his back. Paul called Jeff's name and touched his shoulder. Only another week of school before Jeff could sleep late. Paul shook the shoulder gently. Jeff's ability to sleep through even the worse noise still astounded his father. Jeff opened an eye and his dad left; hearing the shower start on the second floor, he knew Brian was up.

Paul returned upstairs to his own room to finish dressing and continue his morning routine. Fifteen minutes later, after carefully knotting his tie, he went to the safe in the closet and unlocked it. He took out his gun, checked it carefully, strapped on his holster, and grabbed his wallet with the star in it.

Jeff sat at the kitchen table reading a library book. Brian, hair still damp, stood at the stove. He poured beaten eggs into the pan and sprinkled cut-up spinach onto them. He asked, "There's a party at David's tonight. I'll be out late. Okay?"

Paul took the orange juice out of the refrigerator and placed it on the table. He eyed his sixteen-year-old son critically. "Who's supervising the party? Remember you have to pick up your brother by midnight. I'll be late."

"Dad! Nobody's going to do drugs or drink. We're not going to have an orgy on the carpet!"

"What's an orgy?" Jeff asked.

"When people enjoy themselves more than they imagine," his father answered the ten-year-old. He turned back to Brian. "Are David's parents going to be home?"

His son grinned at him, "I think they're the ones supplying the condoms."

"I know what a condom is," Jeff said. "I saw it on TV."

"As long as your bother knows, is what's important," Paul said.

Paul squeezed behind Jeff's chair to get to the drawer with the utensils. He found the silverware, placed it on the table, and grabbed a coffee cup. The kitchen sat at the back of the house with a window overlooking the cluttered back porch and small urban back yard.

Brian's voice squeaked as he began to speak. "I promise to clean the basement and the attic the first day of vacation."

"You have to clean them anyway. You usually don't resort to bribery until after you've whined for ten minutes. You in a rush?"

"My whine quotient got used up talking to Coach yesterday. He expects us to do a full workout in this heat, *besides* regular practice."

"Just remember to drink lots of fluids and you should be okay," Turner said.

Paul and his sons ate breakfast together every weekday. They

2

rose a half hour early to share at least the one meal together, to talk, compare schedules, settle family squabbles. Paul Turner's workday started at eight thirty, and as much as he tried to stick to a set schedule, the amount of overtime required of a detective in Area Ten of the Chicago Police Department made this almost impossible. In spring Brian's baseball practice kept him out until six most nights. Jeff's schedule varied because of his physical therapy. Paul wanted them together at least once a day for a meal one of them cooked. They each took a week and rotated assignments. One cooked, one set the table, one cleaned up. Jeff's meals were, understandably, simple. The kitchen had special chairs, hooks, and pulleys to aid Jeff, although Turner stood ready to help and often assisted Jeff if things got complicated.

On the car radio on the way to work, the announcer gave the temperature as eighty-one degrees. The National Weather Service predicted another record high temperature in Chicago, with little chance of a break in the early-June heat wave.

As usual, the detectives in Area Ten mumbled their way through Friday-morning roll call. The structure they sweated in was south of the River City complex on Wells Street, in a building as old and crumbling as River City was new and gleaming. Fifteen years ago the department had purchased a four-story warehouse scheduled for demolition, and decreed it would be the new Area Ten headquarters. To this day rehabbers occasionally put in appearances. In fits and starts the building had changed from an empty hulking wreck to a people-filled hulking wreck. The best that could be said about it was that the heat usually worked in winter. The worst was that it had absolutely no air conditioning.

Sergeant Felix Specter had been through roll call with some of them over a thousand times. They rested their back ends on folding chairs. The bulletin board hung to the left of the chalkboard in front of the room. Messages crammed the entire surface. Turner glanced over the items on the board: the usual

3

announcements of retirement parties and a few notes from the Fraternal Order of Police, the cop union in Chicago. Next to the bulletin board hung the chart of acceptable hair lengths in the department.

Later in the squad room, Paul joined his partner, Buck Fenwick, at the coffee machine. Buck was on another diet. They'd been partners five years and Buck had gained an average of eight pounds per year.

"Double and triple fuck," Buck swore as he shook the last grains of sugar from a mangled box.

Turner said, "I thought you couldn't have sugar on the new diet."

"I get ten grains a cup." He shook the box again.

Ten years ago the Chicago Police Department created Area Ten to combat the rising wave of crime along Chicago's lake front. It ran from Fullerton Avenue on the north to Fifty-fifth Street on the south, and from Lake Michigan west to Halsted Street.

Turner took his black coffee, strolled to his desk, and began sorting through files, active cases to be pursued today, leftover paperwork from an ax murder in Grant Park. From the start Paul had been sure it was the deranged father-in-law who'd done it. They had caught the guy two nights earlier trying to retrieve the ax from the bottom of Buckingham Fountain. Unfortunately for him the police had found the ax already and had set up watchers in case he returned.

Buck Fenwick arrived at his desk, which was front-to-front with Turner's, and threw himself into his chair. Turner heard the telltale squeaks of protest that told him the chair had about another week and a half before Fenwick's bulk would crush it to the floor. Fenwick perched the cup on a stack of files, as he always did. Coffee sloshed out, as it always did. Turner handed him a napkin, as he usually did. "Double fuck," Fenwick swore, mopping it up.

Turner liked being partnered with Fenwick. They could hardly have been more different. Turner's dark haired five feet eleven inches contrasted with the blond bulk of his rapidly

4

balding friend. Fenwick didn't sweat the small stuff. Turner appreciated his casualness.

Sergeant Specter bustled into the squad room, his white shirtsleeves already rolled up past the elbow, revealing the angry red flaking that started with the first seriously humid days of the Chicago summer. No doctor had been able to cure it and neither mounds of salve nor special-ordered ointments seemed able to control it. He slapped a message on Turner's desk.

"Oak Street Beach, and you better hurry." He moved off quickly.

Turner and Fenwick took one of the old unmarked Plymouths from the lot. They crossed Congress Parkway and turned left to descend to Lower Wacker Drive, a little-used but extremely efficient method of crossing the Loop without the usual hassle of masses of pedestrians and blocks of jammed traffic. Fenwick drove with a cab driver's abandon. He claimed city driving was just like bumper cars when he was a kid going to carnivals. Turner always hooked his seat belt and spent the time watching the passing scenery. They parked illegally across from the Drake Hotel and took the pedestrian underpass to the beach.

Near the children's play area, just north of Oak Street Beach about fifty feet from the LaSalle Street off-ramp, the beat cops had roped off an area one hundred by one hundred feet. Joggers slowed to crane their necks at the mob of cops trudging around in the sand next to the jungle bars. As he plodded through the sand, Turner observed a tall blond man who looked to be in his mid-sixties sitting on a park bench. The man let tears stream from his eyes, making no attempt to stanch the flow. He occasionally wiped at his upper lip with the back of his hand.

A beat cop named Mike Sanchez met Turner and Fenwick half way across the sand. Turner knew Sanchez and liked him. Recently Sanchez had taken the detectives test, and Turner asked him if he'd gotten the results. He got a shrug and a no.

Sanchez explained. "We got big problems here. This guy," he

jerked his thumb toward the crier," is the Reverend Bruce Mucklewrath."

He hardly needed to say more. Not only did Mucklewrath have a national reputation, but his distinguished face had been plastered all over every TV station in the Chicago area for the past three weeks. He was on a campaign fund–raising and religious tour, gathering money from and speaking to the faithful. He'd just finished his first term as senator from California, and was in the middle of a brutal campaign to get himself reelected.

Prior to his election, his fame had rested securely on a far-flung spiritual and financial empire. His critics scoffed at the missions he funded for the homeless in every major city in the country, saying they were only for show. The voters in the state of California had elected him senator in a freak three-way race. The Republican and Democratic candidates had split the middle-of-the-road and minority votes almost evenly. The far right had spent thirty million in the most expensive senatorial campaign ever. The reverend, as an independent, had won by slightly less than two thousand votes out of eleven million cast.

Turner had read a couple of Mucklewrath's speeches and followed his career, as had most Americans. He didn't like him. As a rookie cop, Turner had learned to put his emotions on cruise control during an investigation. He'd lost his temper a few times after becoming detective. The last time was when he'd gone after a drug dealer who'd murdered an entire family— father, mother, and three kids all under the age of five—because the father was behind in his payments. His temper outburst had caused the dealer to have an unfortunate encounter with a brick wall. The defense attorney used it to escape, his client getting a penalty only a little more inconvenient than a trip to the dentist. Turner had learned: add your temper to personal feelings and nowadays you lose a perfectly good bust.

"What happened?" Turner asked.

"We got a dead body over there." Sanchez pointed to a jungle-gym set. "The reverend hasn't been able to tell us much. Pretty broken up. We do know it's his daughter."

As the three of them stepped toward the children's play area Sanchez said, "We got a visit from one of the people in the mayor's office. This is going to get political."

"I suppose it will." Turner sighed.

Close up now, they saw the mass of twisted blond hair streaked with red splayed out on the sand. The body lay six inches from one of the metal struts supporting the jungle gym. Sunlight gleamed on the metallic surfaces of the eight-foot-tall children's play set. Remnants of the disaster clung to the light-blue summer dress the victim wore. Bits of brain, blood, and gore covered the sand next to the nonexistent face.

Sanchez pointed to a small cluster of people thirty feet to the north of the body. "They're as close as we've got to witnesses. No one saw the actual shooting. They all showed within minutes."

Fred Nokosinski was clambering up the play set to get pictures from above. A bearded dwarf, Fred always took the crime-scene photos. He grunted a hello down toward them. The white van with CHICAGO CRIME LAB printed on the side had been driven over the sand to the crime scene. Paul saw a tall, young, new guy he didn't know fussing with materials in the back of the van. Two feet from the body Sam Franklin, the head of this crime-lab unit, knelt in the sand. He held a thin piece of screen boxed by four wooden slats. Through this he carefully sifted grains of sand, hunting for evidence. Two other men around the body engaged in the same activity.

Sam rose and greeted the detectives.

"Be a miracle if we find anything in this sand," he said. "You guys are going to be up to your tits in politics in this one. Know who the dad was?" Turner thought he sounded altogether too confident and cheerful.

Turner nodded. "Any idea what happened?"

"I can get you all the technical details later. For now, somebody blew her away. No weapon around." He nodded toward the lake. "Lots of room to toss a gun." He glanced toward Mucklewrath. "They haven't been able to get the preacher to talk, which I guess is unusual for him." Sam shrugged. "I don't envy you guys."

"We'll call you later," Turner said. He and Fenwick walked to

7

the bench and sat on either side of the Reverend Mucklewrath. Turner eyed him warily. One of the first lessons they taught you was, always watch the family most carefully. In all likelihood, if one of them hadn't done it, one of them knew something about why.

Turner watched the man pulling in vast gulps of air and exhaling them noisily. Sand covered his black wing-tip shoes, the knees of his pants, and his suit coat up to the elbows. His clothes were spattered with blood and gore, concentrated mostly on the front of his shirt and suit coat, probably where he'd held his daughter. Paul pictured the man holding his lifeless child. As the father of a child with spina bifida, he'd held Jeff many a night when he didn't know if the boy would survive an operation. He didn't want to imagine his son dying.

Turner said, "Sir, I know it's difficult, but we need to talk to you, ask you some questions."

After mopping his face with a pink handkerchief, and still breathing erratically, Mucklewrath said, "I want the killers punished." He gasped for air and shuddered. "I want them punished in such a way that they will pay forever, here and in hell."

"Yes, sir, I understand," Turner said. "You could help us catch them if you could answer a few questions."

"Who would want to hurt her? Such a good and beautiful daughter. Her angelic smile. She laughed so beautifully. So full of life and hope."

Turner said, "Please, sir, a few questions."

He mopped his face again and stuck the hankie in his suit-coat pocket. "All right."

"Could you tell us what happened?" Turner asked.

Speaking with numerous pauses and gasps for air, the reverend told them that he liked to bring his daughter on his speaking trips. His wife usually came, too, but this time had stayed to oversee some changes in the new university their ministry was building in Laguna Beach. Today the Reverend Mucklewrath didn't have a meeting until ten. So when his daughter expressed a desire to go out together for an early walk, they chose a stroll along the shore. "We've been here before. It seems so safe in the middle of Oak Street Beach. All the people going by on Lake Shore Drive."

A few tears escaped his eyes. Paul thought they were real, but he'd discovered over the years that some killers were often completely overcome with grief after they'd murdered.

The reverend continued, "She was so happy, so content. We talked about her new role in the upcoming campaign. She'd finished her sophomore year in college and wanted to spend the summer helping me. She had plans and dreams. Real ideas to help out. A father couldn't expect more from a child." As he finished the sentence he broke down sobbing.

The cops waited patiently. Turner noted that the bench sat in a grassy area about ten feet from the jungle gym and about thirty feet from the shore. The leaves of a few trees let in the dappled sunlight on what should have been a peaceful patch of quiet earth. None of the bathers who would cram the beach by noon were around to see horror on this beautiful morning.

The reverend resumed. "She's been my joy since she was born." He used his sleeve to wipe the tears on his face.

Turner understood. He'd almost lost Jeff several times when the boy was small. He knew the fear and sorrow.

Finally Mucklewrath started again by saying that he hadn't observed many people on the nearly deserted beach. The three men had come up from behind them, so he hadn't seen or heard them.

"Two of them grabbed me. One gripped me around the neck. I tried to struggle. He tightened his arm. I nearly passed out. Another one held a knife to Christina's throat while grabbing her from behind. I thought they meant to rob us. Then one of the men holding me pulled out a gun. He swung it . . ." He paused and gasped for breath, then continued. "He swung it toward Christina. She couldn't see the gun from the way the evil piece of filth held her. Then I saw . . ." His voice fell to a whisper. "I'll never forget it."

Turner expected an emotional crack, but the reverend talked on almost as if he were in a trance.

"The one holding me said, 'This is your last look at happiness.' The other raised the gun. Aimed. The silencer muffled the noise. The bullet . . ." He stopped for several moments. "I struggled mightily. I tried to cry out. The one holding me squeezed my throat tight enough so that I passed out. The last thing I remember him saying is 'Sorry now, aren't you?' They left enough life in me so I could come back to this horror."

"We're sorry for your loss," Turner said.

The man nodded. Turner and Fenwick waited for him to regain control.

Finally Fenwick asked, "You're sure he said, 'Sorry now, aren't you'?"

"Yes."

"Why would he say that?"

"I don't know."

"Can you tell us more about your attackers?" Fenwick asked.

The reverend looked at Fenwick through bleary eyes. "It all happened so quickly," he said.

"Were they white, black, Hispanic?" Turner asked.

"White, I think. They had masks on. It was hard to tell much about them."

"Do you remember anything about what they wore? Jogging outfits or dress clothes?"

"They wore street clothes. I think one wore dress pants, the others jeans. I think they had on sport coats. Dark colored. I don't remember."

"Shoes?"

"I didn't notice. Most of the time I was looking at Christina and talking or listening to her."

"Even the smallest thing," Turner prompted. "Maybe the color of hair?"

Mucklewrath thought a minute. "No. Sorry. I didn't pay attention."

Turner knew the answer to the next question, but he knew he had to ask it anyway. "Reverend, do you have any enemies?"

Bruce Mucklewrath's answer to such a question could have filled a Chicago telephone book, white and yellow pages combined. *Time* magazine had done a cover story about the death threats that became a central theme of the Reverend's California campaign. He'd viciously attacked any group even slightly to the left of his own positions.

The preacher said, "Doing the Lord's work can cause unreasoning hatred in those who haven't yet seen the light."

The sanctimoniousness of the reply grated on Turner's nerves, but he didn't let this show as he said, "I meant anyone in particular. Any specific threats?"

"No. None. I can't believe anyone would do such a thing."

They asked numerous other questions, but got no further information. Fenwick said, "That's all for now, Reverend. It we think of anything, we'll get in touch."

"Catch them, punish them. I can feel the Lord calling for vengeance."

They left after assuring him they'd do their best to catch the killers.

"He's gotta know more," Fenwick said.

"Give him time," Turner said. "We can get an enemies list and check it to see if anybody's in town. We can find out if anybody in Califorina's got a comprehensive list of the threats, what they found, if anything. Let's try the witnesses."

As they walked up the beach Turner was grateful for the coolness of the nearby water. He could feel sweat trickling down the back of his neck.

Fenwick said, "I wonder if anybody on the Drive saw anything as they went by."

"The guardrail pretty much blocks the view," Turner said, "and it's over fifty feet away. Who'd be paying attention during rush hour? Probably nobody, but we'll have to check it out, if we can."

"They must have been cool heads," Fenwick said, "to try something this bold. How'd they know they wouldn't be interrupted or chased? Their exits are limited. Up or down the beach, through the tunnel the way we came in, or a dash across six lanes of traffic on the Drive." Fenwick paused. "Maybe they had a boat waiting," he suggested.

"Let's try our witnesses," Turner said.

The meager group of four witnesses chatted sporadically with each other. A uniformed police officer hovered nearby so none of them would give in to the urge to walk off.

The two women in their fifties, dressed in red shorts, walking shoes, and Chicago Bears T-shirts, and wearing Walkman radios, explained that they hadn't heard or seen anything, but had come upon the unconscious reverend and tried to revive him. One woman had bright red hair that didn't look dyed. The other had black hair that could only have come from a bottle and which she had tied back in a ponytail.

"We didn't see the body until a minute later," the black-haired one said.

"The sand kind of hid her," said the red-haired one.

"We were shocked. I never want to see such a thing again," the first woman said.

"Which way did you come from?" Turner asked.

"Lake Point Towers," said the redhead. They hadn't passed anyone on their walk up from the south.

Neither had approached the body. They hadn't seen any boats in the water. After a few more questions, which elicited no further facts, Turner and Fenwick moved on to a young jogger who couldn't have been much over eighteen. His blue and white Chicago Cubs T-shirt still clung to his torso in wet patches. His gauzy jogging shorts fit snugly around his ass and crotch. Paul doubted he wore a jockstrap, but thought he probably should have.

The boy's name was Frank Balacci. "I was jogging down from Fullerton. I saw the women and then I spotted something near the kids' play area. I walked up to the body." His face turned pale as it must have done at the time. "I didn't get close, but near enough. I tossed my cookies into the lake. I left the body and came to help the women here. Then I ran to call the cops." He hadn't noticed anyone suspicious on his run from the north, definitely not three men together. He'd had a clear view of the lake as he jogged. "Definitely no boats around anywhere," he told them.

"That eliminates three directions," Fenwick said as they turned to the last witness.

This was a tall thin man with completely gray hair. Even on

so warm a day, he wore a sweater and a white shirt buttoned to the collar. Two Afghan hounds sat placidly on either side of him, their leashes held firmly in his right hand. His lisp had to be practiced. Turner noted a large gap between the man's upper two front teeth.

"I'm a retired architect," he explained. "I walk along here every morning at precisely this time. Look at the skyline behind you. I had a hand in designing a significant number of the buildings you are looking at. I own small portions of many of them."

His name was Alexander Polk and he'd seen something. "I'd just emerged from the underpass by Oak Street when these men walked past me. I knew something was furtive about them. They moved too fast to be out for a pleasant stroll. They weren't dressed for jogging, and they weren't any of the regulars down here. Very suspicious." He'd paid them little heed after that. Polk could only tell the police he thought they all had dark hair and were white. He couldn't remember the color of their clothes and hadn't stopped to watch where they went. He hadn't seen any others. Polk had then proceeded up the beach and come upon the scene as described by the others.

None of the witness had seen anyone else. The beach, sparsely traveled at this hour on a weekday, didn't lend itself to eyewitnesses; that was probably why the killers used this time to strike. After taking down the witnesses' addresses, Turner and Fenwick told them they could go.

Fenwick looked at the high-rises that lined Lake Shore Drive. He sighed despondently. "Maybe someone up there saw something."

"We'll need to get some help canvassing all those places," Turner said.

The case sergeant, who rarely showed up at a crime scene, approached them from across the sand. Prominent people drew official concern the way shit draws flies. Turner treated each case the same, or as nearly as he could. He figured they were all crimes to be solved. It shouldn't matter who was involved, whom he liked or disliked. He had a job to do.

The sergeant looked concerned. This was the face he used

when out in public where a reporter or a civilian might see him. He delayed their investigation with exhortations to work hard, cover all bases, interview everybody.

With this rush of interest, Turner got him to commit an extra four people for the canvass of the high-rises.

The crowd on the beach had been reduced to a few of the desperate or bored, hoping for some kind of excitement. By this time the pictures had been taken, the schematic drawing of the scene had been made, the fingerprints on the jungle gym had been lifted. A team of men working in large roped-off squares of beach carefully sifted through the sand hunting for any kind of evidence that might lead to the identity of the killers. They would be doing it for a fifty-foot radius around the scene. Turner didn't think they'd find much.

Turner tapped his pen on his standard-issue blue notebook. He'd set in clean paper this morning before he left. Seeing eight people grouped around the Reverend Mucklewrath, he nudged Fenwick, and they strolled over.

The reverend stared fixedly at where police personnel worked around his daughter's body.

As they neared the group, Fenwick said, "This had to be extremely well planned, or these guys were really lucky. A jogger, a casual stroller, anybody could have come along and seen everything, or the good reverend is making the whole story up."

"I'd thought about that," Turner said. "We'll have to see, although our last witness confirms the three suspicious characters."

When they got within ten feet of Mucklewrath, a tall man in a dark-gray suit and tie left the crowd and walked to them. "I'm Dr. Hiram Johnson, the spokesperson for the Reverend Mucklewrath. If you need to know anything, I'll be able to help."

Fenwick said, "We'll need to talk to all the people staying with the Mucklewrath party."

Dr. Johnson patted the front of his buttoned suit coat. "It is much more normal for me to deal with the public and any questions."

Turner eyed the man's bald head, which gleamed in the bright June sunlight. Johnson looked totally comfortable in his suit.

1 4

Turner wished he could take off his own sport coat and loosen his tie, but especially take off his shoes and socks. He could feel the grit of the sand that had seeped into them.

"Dr. Johnson," Fenwick said, "this is a murder investigation. We talk to whoever we want whenever we need to."

Dr. Johnson did not become indignant as Turner expected. Instead he installed a bland unctuous look on his face. The man said, "I did not mean to imply that I was interfering. I simply meant to be as helpful as possible. Anyone in the Reverend Mucklewrath's organization is ready to assist the police at this tragic moment."

"Where were you this morning, Dr. Johnson?" Fenwick asked.

"In my hotel room. Making phone calls for the next cities the tour will be in. Setting up last-minute details."

"Can you provide us with a list of those calls?" Fenwick asked. They could get them from the hotel easily enough.

"I'd be happy to, Officer."

By the time half Fenwick's question was asked, Turner knew his partner didn't like the guy either.

If Dr. Johnson noticed, he didn't let on.

"Where are you all staying?" Fenwick asked finally.

Johnson pointed across Lake Shore Drive to a building several doors down from the Drake Hotel. "We have several suites at the Oak Street Arms, all interconnected."

"Do they look down on the beach here?" Fenwick asked.

"Yes. And no, I didn't happen to look out. As far as I know, no one did. We didn't learn of this until a policeman came up a few minutes ago. We all rushed down here."

"Do you know who might have wanted to hurt the Reverend? Someone who held a grudge?" Fenwick asked.

Dr. Johnson spread his hands out flat, palms up. He said, "The Reverend had many enemies. I'm sure we'll have a statement available later. There are many servants of Satan who are capable of great evil."

Turner said, "I remember the *Time* magazine article on the threats in the Senate campaign. Can you tell us anything about them, especially if any new threats had been made in the past week or so?"

"None that I know of. You'll have to talk to Donald. He deals with the Reverend's security." They asked Johnson a few more questions, but he was no further help.

Johnson beckoned over another man. He introduced him as Donald Mucklewrath, son of the preacher and head of security.

Donald Mucklewrath wore an impeccable gray suit and a grave frown. He dismissed Johnson with a nod, then shook hands with both cops. The son had to be in his thirties.

"We're sorry about your sister's death," Turner said.

"Thank you," he said softly. Tears sprang from his red-rimmed eyes.

Fenwick said, "We realize this is a difficult time, but we need to check a few things with you. You didn't happen to look out a window this morning and see anything?"

"No. I usually sleep late. We don't finish with the security checks after each prayer meeting until two or three in the morning. We're very thorough. I didn't know anything until your men came to the suite."

"How does the Reverend's security work?" Turner asked.

"Not good enough. If you don't catch whoever did this, I'm sure there'll be a network of righteous volunteers prepared to step forward to avenge my sister's death."

"I meant," Turner said, "the practical details. How many of you are there? That kind of thing."

The younger Mucklewrath told them that the permanent staff consisted of himself and three others. They worked in shifts, accompanying the Reverend on official business and always on the podium at his talks and prayer meetings. In each city they supplemented their numbers from among the faithful and sometimes the local police.

Turner eyed him curiously. At about six feet, Donald Mucklewrath stood an inch or so taller than Turner. His blond hair was swept back from his face, ending in slight curls that stopped at the edge of his suit-coat collar. His suit didn't try to hide his muscularity.

Fenwick said, "What you're saying is that normally someone would not accompany the Reverend and his daughter on a morning walk like this."

The younger Mucklewrath moved closer to them. Turner could smell the tang of recently used mint, probably toothpaste, on his breath. The son said, "My father wanted to live as normal a life as possible. He is one of the people. He thought going around with a security detail every minute offended the Lord. My father put his faith in God."

"Then what were you for?" Turner asked.

"Satan can have human agents. Mostly I am in charge of sweeps of public places. We've had many bomb threats. We thoroughly examine every place the week before, then the day before, and then finally do a sweep just before my father starts to preach. Everyone who comes to one of my father's prayer sessions has to pass through a metal detector. All packages are searched."

"'Prayer sessions'?" Fenwick asked.

"That's what my father likes to call his meetings with his people and God."

"Do you find much in your searches?" Turner asked.

"Seldom. Believers come to hear the word. His enemies stay away. Are you saved?"

Fenwick raised an eyebrow. "We prefer to discuss what happened, Mr. Mucklewrath."

"Of course, but you should consider accepting Jesus Christ as your savior. It's his guidance at times like this that helps one pull through."

Fenwick said through gritted teeth, "Does your father usually take walks in the morning?"

"Not often, but Christina sometimes insisted and my father could seldom refuse a request of hers. He always said she was an angel sent from heaven."

"How old was Christina?" Turner asked.

"Twenty-one next month. I'll be thirty-two in a week. We were half-brother and sister. My father divorced my mother twenty-five years ago."

17

"Where is Christina's mother?" Fenwick asked.

"She died in a plane crash fifteen years ago."

Turner asked. "Where is your mother?"

"Who cares? She was an unbeliever. She turned on my father."

"And the current Mrs. Mucklewrath? The Reverend said—"

Donald interrupted. "She's back in California organizing part of Father's next legislative agenda and several other matters. We called. She's taking the family jet and will be here in a few hours."

The son knew of no specific new threats. "They happen a lot during the election campaign. There are always crazy people around. Those who do the Lord's work are often hated." He repeated Johnson's promise of a statement later.

"Had your father or your sister seemed more worried or fearful lately? Acted in any way unusual?" Fenwick asked.

"My father fears no man or beast," Donald said. "He's been his usual self. No problems. Never happier. We'd prayed together as usual at dinner last night. He was looking forward to a successful run in Chicago. Soldier Field is sold out for the next seven nights."

Better than most rock concerts, Turner thought.

Mucklewrath continued, "My sister has been in the best of spirits."

"Will the reverend still go on tonight?" Turner asked.

"Yes, definitely. He will pray with his people for the soul of his daughter and the destruction of the evil seed who have spawned this hideous tragedy."

He had no further useful information for them.

As they got in their squad car to drive off, Fenwick asked, "Do they always talk like they're addressing the multitudes?"

Turner said, "I don't know. I've never been a multitude before."

TWO

The ruts on Wells Street south of River city nearly ripped the guts out of their unmarked car. Fenwick's tendency to drive twenty miles over the speed limit didn't help. On principle, he refused to change his mode of driving to accommodate a road. They drove around a crew of city workers standing and staring at numerous potholes in the street, and almost tripped on a heap of new construction materials piled next to the steps leading into the station.

Wilmer Pinsakowski, resident bum and would-be snitch, caught them just inside the door. In June, with the temperature hovering near ninety at noon, he had completely opened his overcoat. At his throat tufts of hair peeked over his three shirts. Every Friday Wilmer shaved and smelled as if he'd been doused with men's cologne. This was his concession to cleanliness. Turner was sure he hadn't bathed since the first Mayor Daley's administration.

Fenwick growled at Wilmer and tried to brush past him. Wilmer clutched at their coats. "I know who killed that preacher's daughter," he said.

"Wilmer, it's not good to lie about important things. What happened last time?" Fenwick asked.

Wilmer whimpered. For a couple of months, when Wilmer first showed up at the station six years ago, they had followed up all his tips. All of them had led to nothing, and they'd given up listening to him. Then, early this year, Wilmer'd insisted his tip in an important case was true. Turner and Fenwick decided to give it a try. They staked out an abandoned church on south State Street. It turned bitterly cold that day and before the night passed it began to snow. No crook appeared and Fenwick caught pneumonia. As revenge Fenwick had taken Wilmer to a detox clinic and it had almost killed the old guy.

"I just want to help," Wilmer said.

"You need to get out of here, Wilmer, before the lieutenant sees you. You know what he said last time."

Wilmer whimpered again and began to shuffle toward the door. Fenwick, now at the booking desk, asked loudly, "What the hell you letting in that fuckhead for? You new here?"

The young cop at the desk flushed red. "Sorry, but he said he knew something about the murder. I didn't know."

"Well, keep him the fuck out of here." Fenwick took the stairs to the second floor two at a time.

Turner patted Wilmer on the shoulder and pointed to the lieutenant descending the stairs on the far side of the room. He said, "You better go. The lieutenant was awful mad last time he caught you in here."

Wilmer nodded and staggered toward the door.

In the squad room a few minutes later, Turner observed Roosevelt and Wilson arguing about the merits of various bug sprays. Roosevelt and Wilson had been detectives since the year one. Joe Roosevelt, red-nosed, with short, brush-cut gray hair and bad teeth, and Judy Wilson, an African-American woman with a pleasant smile, had a well-deserved reputation as one of the most successful pairs of detectives on the force. Despite this, they averaged a major squabble about a senseless issue at least once a week. It usually started with something minor and stupid and ended with them in pouty silence. As soon as they started a new case, they shrugged off the problem. Anyone observing this stage of their relationship would have thought they were best friends, which in fact they were.

Paul Turner draped his coat over the chair behind his desk. Fenwick turned on the fan that sat on the filing cabinet behind his desk. The breeze barely made a dent in the sweat that began to form in his armpits. He wished they'd rehabbed the air conditioning first when they decided to redo the building.

They'd spent the bulk of the morning, after the interviews on the beach, knocking on doors in the high-rises along Lake Shore Drive. Out of twenty-three doors that had been answered, they'd learned nothing. They'd have to return to check the fourteen that didn't answer. The other men from the squad, who'd been to the other buildings, reported similar findings.

They talked to Dean Fox, the cop who had helped the witness Alexander Polk look at mug shots and had drawn the composite sketch based on Polk's memory. Fox said, "We spent an hour and a half on the mug shots. He didn't recognize anybody. We might have somebody new here."

He showed them the sketches he and Polk had worked on. "Not much," Fox said.

Turner and Fenwick agreed: The drawings could have been of half a million different people.

Turner took out some of the paperwork forms from the bottom drawer of his desk.

He inserted the Daily Major Incident Log form into his typewriter. He typed in the time in military hours. In the crime/incident column he typed Homicide/Murder.

"I heard it's a doozy," bellowed a far-too-friendly voice.

Turner didn't even look up from his typing.

He knew the voice belonged to the relentlessly cheerful newest member of the squad, Randy Carruthers, a fresh-faced young man whose tight clothes indicated recently gained weight. Frequently he carried at least one catalogue from a law school. He talked most often about taking law courses, so he could "get out of this hell hole and get a real job." Turner wished him all the luck in the world. He occasionally thought of secretly writing to every law school in the state for catalogues and giving them to Carruthers. On the other hand, as of yet, Paul had seen no evidence of law or any other type of classes taken or passed. He ignored Carruthers and kept working.

Fenwick got busy putting the paperwork and other details of their current cases up to date and on hold. The sergeant had told them to drop everything else and work on this one. Turner finished the basics on the Major Crime Worksheet for the case and began making phone calls.

He called the Eighteenth District police station to check on the frequency and regularity of patrols on the beach. The desk sergeant told him they seldom bothered with the beach that early in the day.

Turner hung up and told Fenwick what he'd learned.

Fenwick said, "Mucklewrath doesn't have a regularly scheduled morning walk. No regularly scheduled patrols by the cops. So the killers took a random chance. Saw an opportunity and took it."

Turner said, "I like your idea of being suspicious of the Reverend. Only he could have timed it perfectly."

Fenwick said, "Yeah, maybe. Let's keep checking." Each reached for a phone.

It was one o'clock Chicago time, only eleven in the morning in California. Since Mucklewrath lived and had his main office in Los Angeles, Turner called police headquarters there. He explained his purpose and was transferred fairly quickly to a Sergeant Dooley.

Turner said, "I'm working on a homicide. I don't know the Reverend Mucklewrath or his people. Any help you can give me, I'd sure appreciate."

The voice on the other end said, "The most frustrating people I've ever dealt with. Investigating the threats they claimed to get was the most god-awful case. I got absolutely nothing." She gave an exasperated sigh.

"Nobody caught?"

"Nobody even suspected."

"No leads?" he asked.

She snorted. "I'm saying not a nibble."

22

"I don't understand."

Dooley said, "Nobody ever got suspected because we could never even prove they got the calls."

"They didn't order a tap?"

"Nope. I suspect they were more afraid of police finding out information about their group than they were about catching bad guys. This next is between you and me. If you repeat it, I'll call you a liar."

Turner grunted agreement.

Dooley said, "I have my doubts that they ever got such calls. I think it was a political ploy to get sympathy from the voters."

"You investigated?"

"Sure. You ever try to get information from those guys?"

"Just this morning from a Dr. Johnson and the son."

"Didn't get much, did you?"

"Nope."

Dooley snorted again. "And you won't get much more. That whole crowd is very secretive."

"Would any of them have a motive to kill the daughter?"

Dooley considered this, then said: "They are a tough group. Dedicated, committed. Their cause is all-important. You got kids?"

"Yeah."

"Can you imagine sacrificing your kid at any age for a cause?" Dooley asked.

"No."

"They could. They're nuts. You talk to the current wife yet?"

Turner told her no.

"I doubt if you'll get anything out of her. We call her the 'ice maiden' out here. She's tough as nails and is probably the real brains of the outfit. She's certainly much smarter than the Reverend and his son put together. Behind the scenes she gives the orders. She's got an MBA from Harvard Business School, and she's a CPA."

"What about the first wife?"

"Don't have anything on her. I can check and get back to you."

Turner asked her if she would and thanked her. He hung up and looked at Fenwick. The big man sat with his tie off and shirt unbuttoned. On one corner of his desk he kept a towel, which he periodically applied to his neck and forehead. Turner told him what he found out from California.

Fenwick said, "I knew I didn't like them." He heaved his bulk toward the coffee machine three feet behind his desk and poured a cupful into a mug with DAD in big red letters on the side. The cup had been a gift last Father's Day from his nine-year-old twin daughters. He reseated himself and said, "I got this paperwork shit on the other cases caught up. Nothing that can't wait a few days."

Carruthers sauntered over to the coffeepot, crossed the few feet to Turner, and planted a major portion of his rapidly expanding ass on the corner of Turner's desk. "How's the case going?"

Fenwick said, "Listen you double-fuck numbnuts, don't you have work to do? Where's Rodriguez?"

Harold Rodriguez was Carruthers' long-suffering partner. He'd made no secret of the fact that he'd be happy to take the next rookie who showed up in the squad room as a new partner. This didn't seem to bother Carruthers. Turner liked Rodriguez, a generally silent man who worked methodically and with precision. If he arrested you, you were likely to spend time in jail. He seldom made a mistake.

"He's doing research at Eleventh and State. Something on one of our cases."

Area Ten encompassed the Chicago's First, Eighteenth, Twelfth, and Twenty-first police districts as well as including Chicago police headquarters at Eleventh and State. The districts handled minor crime, crowd control, parking tickets. Chicago hadn't had police precincts since O. W. Wilson came in during the early sixties and began cleaning up the department. The Areas handled major crimes. Eleventh and State handled the bureaucracy. Area Ten's boundaries included the Loop, north Michigan Avenue, the yuppie North Side, the resurgent near

South and West sides, and the slums farther south, ending with the university community in Hyde Park.

Turner liked the diversity, liked being in a world-class city amid the tremor and clamor of millions of people.

"We've got to get to the hotel to talk to Mrs. Mucklewrath," Fenwick said. "She's got to be in by now and if we get time, we can make our callbacks."

Outside, Fenwick growled, "Carruthers is the biggest double fuck in the city. —Correct that." He pointed to their car.

Wilmer Pinsakowski leaned against the passenger side of their much-dented official car. "That shit is a triple fuck."

Paul knew that the highest rating anyone could get in Fenwick's system was "triple fuck." Usually he reserved this sacred category for inept Bears quarterbacks when they threw game-losing interceptions, or Cubs pitchers who walked in winning runs. The system proceeded through three levels of "shit" to the highest "fuck" category.

"He probably secretly owns half the Loop," Turner said.

"Yeah, and Miss America wants to date me," Fenwick said. "I wish the stupid fuck would stay away."

Paul said, "He's harmless."

Wilmer smiled at them as the two approached him. Paul wished he wouldn't do that. The man's ragged and blackened teeth tempted him to switch to Fenwick's opinion.

Wilmer held out something in his hand. "This is for your boy," he said to Paul. Turner saw a mass of metal that might have once been a toy car. Bent, rusted, and missing three wheels, it had to be a pathetic relic of Wilmer's forays into various neighborhood trash cans.

Turner looked into Wilmer's gray-irised, yellow-rimmed eyes and said, "Thank you, I'm sure he'll enjoy it."

Wilmer smiled. "I got more. I'll bring them all. He'll like them."

Turner occasionally got gifts for Jeff from other members of the squad. They'd cared and been concerned from the first. Many, even Carruthers, had been by the house to visit or bring a gift.

2 5

"You do that," Paul said and smiled back.

"I know who killed that preacher's daughter," Wilmer said.

"Who?" Paul asked.

"Let's go!" Fenwick called from inside the car.

"Who?" Paul asked again.

"Forget him." Fenwick tooted the horn in exasperation. Wilmer could bring out the worst in Fenwick very quickly. "The stupid double fuck couldn't even find the lake if he walked due east from here. Let's go."

"Tell me," Paul said.

But Wilmer was mad now. He pointed his bony new-shaven chin in the general direction of Fenwick. "I ain't gonna tell until he apologizes."

"Good, then we won't have to hear it," Fenwick said from the interior. "Get in the car, Paul."

Near the old drunk, Paul smelled the Friday perfume job. "You see me later," Paul told him.

But the old guy had already begun his obdurate shuffle away from them, and Paul wasn't sure he'd heard.

In the car Fenwick said, "You just encourage him."

"I feel sorry for him," Paul said. "I'm always grateful that I wasn't born a triple fuck like that poor old guy."

"Ah, bullshit."

They drove to the Oak Street Arms and double-parked on the street. Fenwick never had trouble finding a parking place in the city.

A functionary they hadn't met before let them in and directed them through a series of connected suites on the sixth floor to a group of members of the reverend's church clustered around a cluttered dining-room table.

A woman dressed in ice blue with a strand of pearls around her neck glared at them. She sat to the right of the Reverend Mucklewrath, holding a yellow legal-size pad. Turner pegged her as in her mid-thirties, about half her husband's age.

"Who are you and what do you want?" she said before the functionary or Turner or Fenwick could speak.

Donald Mucklewrath whispered in the woman's ear. After a

26

moment she brushed him aside. She nodded a cool greeting and said, "If both of you gentlemen can wait just a minute, I'll be happy to meet you in the living room of the suite just behind you."

Turner and Fenwick waited in a room designed to entertain royalty in the 1890s in India. A Persian rug covered nine tenths of the polished wood surface. Antique chairs and tables formed prim groupings near windows and around fireplaces. Paintings of bucolic landscapes covered three of the walls. On the fourth hung a portrait of some anonymous matron dressed for an evening at the opera.

Mrs. Mucklewrath glided in, yellow legal pad still in hand. The officers greeted her. She sat at the grouping of furniture that overlooked Oak Street Beach. She did not invite them to sit.

She spoke coldly and precisely. "The reverend deeply regrets his decision to take that walk with his daughter. He should have stayed here preparing for meetings. He had numerous fund-raisers to meet and a huge campaign debt to pay back. The members of the Children of God movement have bankrolled him this far. Find those who hated my husband and you'll find the killer.

"Who hated him the most?" Turner asked.

"Read any newspaper. Unbelievers. The shiftless and lazy. Those who wanted a free ride. Everything he fought against."

"I meant any specific individuals," Turner said.

Mrs. Mucklewrath launched into an angry denunciation of those not of their faith, at the end of which they'd learned nothing.

Fenwick tried a different tack. "Could you tell us about you and your husband?"

"We have been married seven years. We are very happy."

Turner tried to picture being married to an iceberg. He said, "What's your relationship with the rest of the members of the organization?"

"I'm in charge. My husband is totally wrapped up in his preaching. He will reach many millions on his mission. I run his business affairs, the university, his election campaign."

"What was your relation with your stepdaughter?" Fenwick asked,.

"I barely saw her. The few times I did, she seemed to be a sweet thing. Her presence gave my husband spiritual comfort. I approved."

Turner did not want to think of what would have happened to the daughter if she didn't approve. Or could she have ordered the murder, because for some obscure reason she didn't approve?

Mrs. Mucklewrath continued, "She was an intelligent woman. We planned a large role for her in the coming campaign. If she did well with that, she could move into the organization soon after she finished college."

"You don't seem upset about Christina's death."

"Someone has to hold this organization together. The men indulge in sniveling excess."

The cops stared at her.

"I will grieve in private, although I will tell you what no one outside the organization knows. For a number of years Christina and I did not get along. Only in the past years has there been some reconciliation. For five years before that I rarely saw her."

"What was the problem between you?" Turner asked.

"She was jealous of my relationship with her father. Very Freudian. She grew up and began to get over it."

"How do you get along with your stepson?"

"He does a competent job. At least he did until today."

"He came from the reverend's first marriage?"

"Right."

"Christina came from his second marriage."

"Yes."

Fenwick asked, "Do you know where the first wife is?"

"I have no idea. She hasn't been in contact with the Reverend Mucklewrath since I've known him."

"Do you know of anyone who would have reason to murder Christina?"

"Our statement should be ready by the time you leave."

28

"How was the reverend's relationship with his daughter?" Turner asked.

The icy glare they got would have stopped a herd of stampeding mammoths in their tracks. She said, "The reverend loved his daughter."

Turner cleared his throat and asked, "About the threats during the senate campaign in California. We'll need lists of names and organizations, anything you have."

"Unfortunately, none of that is available."

"You won't let us have it?" Fenwick asked.

"I'd be happy to give it to you. I'm saying it doesn't exist. What records we kept were destroyed along with the other debris of the campaign."

"Don't you want to catch the people who make the threats?" Turner asked.

"What can such weak and mindless people do?" she asked.

"Murder," Turner said.

For the first time her cold exterior contained a hint of doubt. "We don't have them. Perhaps we should have saved them."

A few minutes later, having gained little information, they rose to leave. Gazing out the window, Turner saw the expanse of beach below. He said, "Anyone looking out the windows this morning could have seen it happen."

"As far as I know, Dr. Johnson and Donald were the only ones in the suite at that hour of the morning."

Turner and Fenwick would have to double-check that statement with the cops who had canvassed the building.

Mrs. Mucklewrath led them back to the room in which they'd seen the others. The reverend stood between Donald and Johnson. He read them the paper in his hand, a press release:

"I am widely hated. Civil libertarians, liberals, communists, anti-Americans, flag burners, criminals, anti–death penalty groups, people on welfare, perverts of every kind. The list is extensive. Those doing the Lord's work must accept the burdens the Lord places on us. The greatest threat to my campaign comes from the godless infidels in San Francisco, my sworn enemies, who have tried to organize boycotts and demonstrations against me, who have tried to disrupt my campaigns and destroy me at every turn. There is where the world will find my daughter's murderer."

Mrs. Mucklewrath said, "That will be released to the press immediately."

Donald let them out. As he did, they asked him if anyone else had been in the suite that morning. He told them no.

In the elevator Fenwick said, "Hell of a statement."

"He's not the first politician who tried to get election mileage out of bashing the gay community."

Downstairs Turner used the phone to call the police district. He wanted to know if any of the other tenants had seen anyone in the rooms or had seen anything suspicious.

He got the squad room and talked to Carruthers. Before Turner could stop him, the overachiever smacked down the phone, after promising to run down to the front desk to see who had been in charge of talking to people at the Oak Street Arms.

While Turner held his hand over the receiver, Fenwick said, "I vote Mrs. M. for the role of evil stepmother in any fairy tale."

Turner shrugged. "Death and grief can cause strange reactions." He listened to distant noises in the station.

Fenwick asked him what the hell was taking so long. Turner explained. "Double fuck" was what Fenwick said.

Finally the answer came back: "Nobody saw anything suspicious."

"Did they talk to the help?" Turner asked.

"They didn't say." Carruthers added, "You know you got a callback from that California cop? That Mrs. Mucklewrath you're looking for? She's in Chicago."

"We know. She flew in about an hour ago. We just talked to her."

"No, no," Carruthers said. "This is the first Mrs. Mucklewrath, the first wife. She lives in Chicago." Carruthers gave them the address.

Turner extricated himself from the conversation a few minutes later. He and Fenwick found the hotel manager and told him they needed to talk to the employees who had any contact with the Mucklewraths.

The manager, Boris Thatcher, a bald man with a minor scar where his harelip had once been, told them what Carruthers hadn't been able to: that the police hadn't interviewed all the help yet; they'd barely finished the guests. "They did tell me that they established that no one saw anyone except the reverend and his daughter enter or leave this morning." The manager added, "Of course, no one was really watching, either. Anyone could have gotten in or out without being seen fairly easily."

Turner heard Fenwick heave a large sigh. Turner said, "For now we'd like to talk to any people who dealt with the Mucklewraths. People who served them meals, that kind of thing."

The manager returned from his office moments later with several lists of people on the shifts for the previous day. He cross-checked the names and jobs and came up with four people. "These are the two maids who would have cleaned their rooms, and these are the two room-service people who would have delivered to their floor, one from each shift last night and this morning."

They caught the two maids just as they were leaving for the day. The Mucklewraths had given no trouble. They'd seen nothing unusual or odd in the Mucklewrath party's behaviors or routines. The maids were used to dealing with demanding guests. The Mucklewraths had been a pleasant change.

Thatcher retrieved the addresses of the two room-service people. Turner and Fenwick stood in the lobby. "Do we see these two now, go talk to the first Mrs. Mucklewrath, or do callbacks?" Fenwick asked.

"Let's see if we can't get the beat cops to do the callbacks." Turner checked addresses. "They're all the hell and gone over the city. Let's try the ex-wife. She's closest."

The heat blasted into them as soon as they left the building. Many times in summer a breeze from the lake saved at least some of the inhabitants of Chicago from the miseries of mind-numbing humidity. Not today. A strong south wind pumped cubic meters of warmth through the city and out over the lake.

Mrs. Mucklewrath lived on School Street just west of Clark. The Cubs had a home game that afternoon, and Turner and Fenwick got caught in the after-game traffic. That they were traveling toward the park instead of away from it helped a little, but what normally would have been a ten-minute trip turned into a half hour of sweat-dripping frustration. "Why don't they air-condition these cars?" Fenwick asked. Turner knew he didn't expect an answer so didn't give one.

They found the address, a town house built within the past two or three years. Besides the numerous freshly painted and rehabbed homes, Wrigleyville had experienced a building boom in housing in the past few years.

They parked in an alley. At the address they found a tiny gray-haired woman plucking weeds from a flowerbed in front of the house. In one hand she flourished a trowel, in the other she held an empty flowerpot.

"Excuse me," Turner said.

The woman straightened up and looked at them. She wore a straw hat, a pair of begrimed work gloves, and a shirt that said MARIGOLD LANES on the back. She smiled at them.

"We're looking for Mrs. Mucklewrath," Turner said.

Her smile became broader. "That's me." She spoke in pleasing, mellow tones.

They showed her their stars.

She invited them into her home, and took them to a sparkling kitchen that overlooked a small backyard with a red brick patio lined with flower beds. After she made them iced tea they sat there in well-cushioned lawn chairs under the shade of an old elm that the builders had found no excuse to destroy.

After they sat down she said, "You're here because that poor child died. I heard it on the noon news."

The officers nodded.

She spoke without prodding. "I've had very little to do with the reverend in nearly twenty years. I haven't missed him. As a husband, he was ghastly. I still marvel that it took me so long to see through him." She shook her head. They had divorced; the settlement left her with half of his property and wealth. "I've managed to live very comfortably because of him. I went back to school. I earned a library-science degree. I volunteer at the local branch a few times a week. I work in my garden. I'm quite content."

"Do you see your son?" Turner said.

"Donald the disappointment? I saw him at the last hearing for the divorce when the decree became final."

"Why don't you see him?" Fenwick asked.

"It's more that he doesn't want to see me. I called him a hypocrite to his face. I brought him up as well as I could in the environment my husband set up. I had far too little influence. I don't lecture the poor lad." She gave a pleasant mirth-filled laugh. "I just tell him the truth about himself and his father. He doesn't like to hear it."

"What truth?" Turner asked. He liked her.

"That the good reverend is in it for the money. God, and the people, and his causes are nice, but it's the amount of cash that comes in that counts. We managed to find many of the hidden bank accounts during the divorce proceedings. I suspect there are lots more."

"They hide money?" Fenwick asked.

She leaned over and patted his knee gently. "Yes, dear. Do you still believe in Santa Claus and the Easter Bunny? I married the man because he was the most handsome and eligible man in Enid, Oklahoma. About the only thing good that came out of the relationship was that he got me away from there. He's got cash coming out of every orifice in his body and stuffed in any number of places. I read the papers. I'm sure the empire continues to grow. If he avoids any major foul-ups, he'll be fine."

"Mrs. Mucklewrath, you mentioned the environment he created," Turner said.

"I went back to my maiden name," she said. "Jill Fondell. Call me Jill."

Turner nodded.

"You asked about environment?" She mused a moment, then her face darkened. She sat forward and spoke quickly and precisely. "Hate. Secrecy. Never trust a soul. Inform on your enemies. Always be suspicious. Above all, Mucklewrath is all-wise, all-seeing, all-good, all full of . . ." Her voice trailed off.

"Are his employees loyal?"

"You must have talked to some. How did they seem to you? Did you get an answer that was of any assistance in your work?"

They shook their heads.

She continued, "I felt very sorry for the daughter. I saw some of the publicity that they managed to get on the newscasts during his campaign six years ago. At every rally the high point was when he trotted out that family. At prayer meetings when Donald was little, he used to hold him on his shoulder at the end. I was so proud then. I'm sure he did the same with the daughter. While we were married, I'd go to every rally, appear on every TV show with him. I was his trophy, his prize."

She smiled and brushed back her gray hair. "Back then I was a size six and spent hours making myself beautiful." She sighed. "You cannot imagine the atmosphere they create around themselves. They pray incessantly. They thank God if they walk through a patch of sunlight. They praise the Lord when the rain starts and when it stops. I doubt if as a little girl she had one minute to play. I doubt if she had any toys, or even a doll. At six years of age they had her on TV preaching! That takes intense coaching. Being perfect at that age must have been hell. Don't be surprised if the solution to your murder is that they sacrificed her for the ultimate publicity coup of the good reverend's career."

Turner asked. "You really think he'd murder his own daughter?"

She considered this carefully before she answered. "He's a bully and a coward in a lot of ways. I doubt if he could pull the

3 4

trigger. Doesn't mean somebody in the organization wouldn't. You met the current wife?"

They nodded.

"I've met her twice. Lovely woman. I'd put my money on her."

"She wasn't in town."

"She could order it done."

In the car Fenwick said, "Could she have done it?"

"The embittered ex-wife?" Turner shrugged powerful shoulders, rotated his neck. "Maybe; I doubt it at the moment. At least she gave us some decent background."

"The whole crowd sounds like a bunch of double fucks. Who would do such things to their kids?"

"Remember she hasn't seen her own in years."

Cubs traffic had let up, but as they drove north to Rogers Park and their next interview they got caught in the heart of rush hour. There'd been a minor accident where Lake Shore Drive ended at Hollywood, and it took them half an hour to get off the Drive.

They found Dirk Lowell, the food-service employee from the hotel, in a second-floor apartment on West Loyola Avenue. He'd been on duty but no one from the Mucklewrath party had requested anything while his shift lasted.

Their last interviewee lived in what used to be Eddie Vrdolyak Tenth Ward, on the far southeast side of the city. Tempted as Fenwick always was to use the siren and put the red flashing light on top of the car, there was little point. It was still rush hour and the backup through Grant Park on Lake Shore Drive wasn't going to move any faster with a cop car squealing and flashing behind it.

Turner made no comment as Fenwick tried to skirt the traffic on the Drive by crossing over to Michigan Avenue. No luck. Another of one of Chicago's many summertime ethnic parades hadn't finished its trek down Michigan Avenue before the required cutoff time. Amazingly Fenwick didn't even get to the double-fuck level the whole time.

Frank Karenski met them at the door of a red brick bungalow on Ninety-second Place. He wore a white muscle T-shirt, cut-off jeans, and no shoes, and he carried a beer. They identified themselves and he let them in. He turned a White Sox game down on the radio and sat with them in the living room. Someone had covered all the major pieces of furniture with wide swatches of clear plastic. Turner felt as if he could slide off any moment.

Karenski apologized for the furniture, saying that with two younger brothers still at home, Mom insisted. "You're lucky they're all out getting hamburgers for dinner," he said.

They explained why'd they'd come.

"Sure," he said. "I brought up a tray of stuff. Around three this morning. Somebody wanted eggs, bacon, and toast, no butter or jelly. And cigarettes. I had to run around to find them because everything in the hotel was closed."

"You're sure about the cigarettes?" Turner asked.

"Yeah. When she called down at that hour, I knew it would be a hassle. Usually it's because somebody's sick. Then I have to run to the drugstore. I keep aspirin and Maalox on hand now. Saves me lots of trips."

"'She'?" Turner said.

"Yeah," Karenski waved his beer at them. "Definitely. Why, is there something wrong with that?"

Turner didn't remember any women besides the daughter being listed among the inhabitants of the suites.

"Who answered the door when you brought the food up?"

"Some guy. An older guy. Maybe in his sixties. I don't know any of those people by sight."

"Bald or blond haired?" Turner asked.

"Bald."

Johnson. They'd need to pay him a little visit.

Fenwick said as they drove back, "Our preacher's group entertained ladies of the evening."

"Or Mrs. Mucklewrath was not in California this morning,"

Turner said, "but I don't see her as the smoking type. Whatever it is, let's get it done. I want to get home."

With rush hour over, the drive back to the Oak Street Arms took only fifteen minutes. They rode up the elevator to the sixth floor and found Johnson among a group just leaving for Soldier Field and that night's rally. The reverend was not with them.

The others left, and the policemen stood in the foyer with Johnson. Fenwick asked the questions. "Who was the woman up here last night?"

Johnson turned slightly pale. "There was no woman," he said.

Fenwick looked bored and disgusted as he asked again, "Who was the woman up here?"

Johnson, pink restored to his cheeks, repeated his denial.

"We got a witness says there was."

"He's lying."

"Let's go to the station and talk about it," Fenwick said.

"What for? You can't do that."

"Sure we can," Fenwick said. "Why can't we?"

Johnson's firm-jawed stare wavered. Suddenly he plopped onto an overstuffed chair. "How did you? You can't tell anyone. Oh, my God."

The officers waited.

"You mustn't tell the reverend. This has nothing to do with him or what happened to Christina. It will only start a scandal. We've never had any scandal about the reverend." He held out his arms to them, pleading. "You won't tell anyone?"

"Convince us why we shouldn't," Fenwick said.

Johnson pulled out a pink silk handkerchief and patted his forehead. He began speaking with the hankie still against his face. "Few people believe this, but the reverend is exactly as he seems. He believes." He took the handkerchief away from his face and gave them a brief look before staring out the window to the lake far below. "He should not suffer because those of us around him are less than perfect. I admit I stray on occasion. My wife never joins us on the reverend's speaking tours. She'd be furious if she knew."

"As angry as the reverend?" Turner asked.

He thought a minute. Finally he said, "I don't know which would be worse. Forgiveness is difficult for the reverend. He expects a great deal of those nearest to him."

"He's gotten rid of other people for these kinds of indiscretions?" Fenwick asked.

"A few. Mostly lower-level staffers. Kids who sign on for the campaigns and don't believe we're serious about enforcing the rules."

"Any top-level people?" Fenwick asked.

Johnson told them, between thorough moppings of his forehead, about a Jason Thurmond, who'd been the Reverend Mucklewrath's campaign coordinator up to his most recent run for office. "It ended in great bitterness, all because the reverend found him in a bar drinking with some reporters."

"Where is he now?" Fenwick asked.

"Thurmond? I don't know."

Turner said, "If the consequences were so severe, how did you have the nerve to bring a woman up here?"

Johnson did another mop with his hankie. Turner thought that if he tried to wring it out, he could add significant moisture to the lake level. Johnson spoke in a voice they could barely hear. "The reverend wasn't here last night. He didn't get in until five this morning. He often goes off by himself in different cities. He leaves and doesn't come back for hours."

"Where does he go?" Fenwick asked.

"I don't know. I doubt if anyone does. Frankly, it's a relief for us to have him gone." He coughed in embarrassment. "Don't misunderstand me. The reverend is a good man, but there aren't many of us who can live up to the moral code he sets for himself."

"We need to talk to the reverend," Turner said.

"He's at the rally," Johnson said.

They listened to his pleas for silence for several minutes, until Fenwick got fed up. He said, "Look, you sniveling little creep. You've got secrets and you need to stop fucking around. Try being honest."

Johnson tried to get indignant, but the cops walked out on his cries of "You can't talk to me that way."

They left without responding.

"Don't lecture me," Fenwick said in the hallway.

Turner said, "About the way you talked to the little weasel? I've got no problem with it."

"Johnson and the ex-wife contradicted each other about what the reverend's in it for," Fenwick said.

"Not the first time a divorced person thought ex-hubby was a piece of shit," Turner said.

Outside Area Ten headquarters they waded through a crowd of reporters demanding answers. Upstairs, the case sergeant said, "We're going to need answers for these reporters soon. What have you got?"

They told Block all they knew. He shook his head. "We're going to need more."

Turner gazed at him levelly. He knew the pressure the sergeant was under, felt some of it himself. People would expect results soon.

Block talked on, giving encouragement along with suggestions for what to do next on the case. They listened with equanimity. Turner knew it was no good losing his temper. The guy was just doing his job.

Finally he left and Fenwick said, "Stupid double fuck. Why doesn't he leave us alone?"

Turner said, "It's useless trying to talk to the reverend tonight. Who knows how long that rally will go for? He'll be talking to thousands. How much of this paper-work you want to do tonight?"

Fenwick gazed at the amount of forms on the top of his desk. He shoved them as you would a pile of particularly odoriferous garbage. "Let's leave this shit until tomorrow."

Turner nodded agreement and they left.

T H R E E

Paul Turner pulled into his driveway just before eight. He walked two doors down Carpenter Street to Gino's grocery on the corner. Summertime strollers filled the sidewalks. Outside the Italian lemon-ice stand people waited in lines four and five deep. In Gino's he nodded hello to Marco behind the counter and loosened his tie as he waited his turn. He ordered a meatball submarine sandwich with extra hot Italian peppers and a large salad. Marco asked after Jeff and Brian. Marco's wife, Maria, gave him a small carton; Paul knew she'd filled it with Italian ice cream. "For Jeffy, he gets around so well."

Paul thanked them and walked around the corner to the house between his and the grocery. Mrs. Rose Talucci lived on the ground floor by herself. Paul loved Rose. She cared for Jeff every day after school whenever Paul or Brian couldn't be home, and often wound up giving the boys and their dad dinner. This was prearranged on a weekly basis. For several years after it started, she refused all offers of payment. Being neighbors, and nearly family, precluded even discussing such things. But one day Mrs. Talucci couldn't fix a broken porch. Paul had offered, and since then he'd done all repairs and had even done several major renovations.

On the second floor of the home lived Mrs. Talucci's two daughters and several distant female cousins. At ninety-one, Mrs. Talucci ruled this brood, her main concern being to keep them out of her way and to stay independent. Numerous times she'd confided in Paul that if they weren't family, she'd throw them all out. She did her own cooking, cleaning, and shopping, as she had for seventy-three years. To her daughter's horror, she took the bus on her own throughout the city and even to suburbs to visit friends, relatives, shopping-center openings, or anything else that struck her fancy as something new and interesting.

She looked up from her copy of Hegel's *Reason in History* and greeted Paul with a friendly nod. Paul gave Jeff a hug and set the ice cream in front of him.

Seeing the carton, Mrs. Talucci said, "That woman is going to spoil the boy."

Jeff said, "Look at my papers, Dad." Every Friday Jeff's teacher put all his work together from the week and sent it home with a progress report for each subject. Paul pulled a chair over and sat next to his son, and they went through each paper, the boy smiling at the many successes, Paul praising him for doing so well or listening to explanations of the few mistakes, making sure his son had understood what he might have done wrong.

Mrs. Talucci stood behind them, leaning against the sink. She saw how the boy leaned against his father, how Paul Turner's arm wrapped around his son's shoulder. She smiled. Such a good father with such nice boys. She crossed herself and prayed for such goodness to continue.

When they finished, Jeff swung himself to the counter and grabbed a spoon and sat back down.

Paul picked up her book, noted the title, and said, "I thought you already had your degree in philosophy."

Casting around for things to do after her husband died, Mrs. Talucci had begun taking courses at the nearby University of Illinois campus. In the past twenty years she'd graduated magna cum laude from three different universities, accumulting one bachelor's and two master's degrees.

She nodded at the book in Paul's hand. "It's for a course down at the University of Chicago. I wanted to brush up a little."

Paul smiled and said, "I have to go out tonight. Can you watch Jeff?"

"I always tell you to go out more. You need to meet someone your own age. You need to be in love. Then you'll be happy."

They'd had this discussion often before.

He said, "I have the boys to look after, and my job."

She interrupted. "No more about the job. You need somebody."

"Marriage—" he began.

"Who said anything about marriage? I know marriage from fifty years with the same man. He was good enough; now I take care of myself. But for a while you need somebody."

Jeff grabbed his crutches and pivoted around the kitchen table and into the living room. Paul heard him turn on the CD player Mrs. Talucci had bought herself as a Christmas present last year. The boy turned on muted music. Paul knew he would later find him curled up with a book.

Mrs. Talucci refilled Paul's glass of lemonade from a plastic container in the refrigerator. She put it in front of him. "I know who you should meet."

Paul held up a hand to protest. "Please."

"He's a nice boy. Ben Vargas. At the garage. The same age as you. A good Italian boy. No paunch and no gray hair. Never been married and Mrs. Pauli thinks he might be, you know."

Paul wasn't sure he was always used to Mrs. Talucci being so open about his sexuality. He'd never told her, but she seemed to know people's secrets before they did. She'd disliked his wife and never made a secret of her feeling that Gail'd been an outsider and not right for him. She'd been trying to fix him up with likely bachelors for years.

She walked over to him, smiling. She moved a chair closer to him at the table, sat down, and patted his arm. "I saw the TV news. That crazy preacher lost his beautiful daughter." She crossed herself. "I knew you'd be late. They always give you the tough cases. You work too hard." She placed her wrinkled old hand on his face. "You're such a good father. You take care of the boys better than any two parents. Go out tonight, enjoy yourself."

He nodded. "I'm a little worried about Brian going to some party tonight."

She smiled. "No need. The party is all innocence. Brian came by earlier. I gave him supper."

"He can make his own," Paul protested. He didn't ask her how she knew about the party and that it would be okay for his son to be there. She would know by her secret ways, and she would be right.

He hurried next door and changed into faded jeans and a black T-shirt. He heard the water running: Brian, undoubtedly, taking another shower. Must want to make a serious impression on some girl, Paul thought. He used the bathroom off his own bedroom to brush his teeth and comb his hair. On his way out he rapped on the door of the bathroom his son used. Brian opened it. Steam rushed out and his son stood there, a towel clutched around his waist.

"Don't be late," Paul told him. "We've got to be up early to get the chores done so we can work on your car."

"No problem, Dad. Maybe we'll have to go to Ben's for an auto part."

"That is not why I want to fix the car. You want to use it, you've got to help fix it and pay for it."

Brian smiled knowingly.

Turner said, "Between you and Mrs. Talucci, you'll have me married off in less than a week." Brian referred to the same Ben Vargas Mrs. Talucci did. Ben had just recently taken over the local garage from his dad, who'd decided to retire. These days Ben was deferential to the point of shyness. Brian had been teasing his dad for weeks. At times Paul thought he caught hints of interest in Ben's eyes. Whenever Paul entered the store, the owner made sure he waited on him. And, to be perfectly honest, Paul had to admit he tried to go there at times he knew Ben was working. Since their cars were old, especially the beater they were fixing up now that Brian turned sixteen, they needed parts quite often.

"Just be home in time to pick up your brother," Paul said.

John Chester's bar sat on lower Wacker Drive where it would have met Madison Street if it had been upper Wacker Drive. Paul parked his car in the dimness and strolled to the door. John Chester's was one of the most popular cop bars in the city. The sinister depths created by shadows and the darkness of the nearby river held little fear for patrons. The bar's reputation kept possible problems in other parts of the city.

John Chester kept the outside immaculately clean, the sidewalk swept, the picture window washed at least once a day on the outside. The room opened out to the left. Rare patrons complained about the dark gloominess of the interior until they glimpsed the mural painted over the left-hand wall from the front all the way to the back. It looked like an Italian Baroque nightmare. Cherubs and praying nuns abounded on hills and fields, amid enough animals to stock half the zoos in the world. More than one drunk had added splashes of color to corners and crevices of the painting, so that parts had faded erratically.

Those in the know ignored the decor and watched the patrons. If they observed carefully, they would see a procession of local, state, and national politicians. One might stop first in the Chicago mayor's office to get an endorsement, but one always stopped at John Chester's in the hope Chester would give his nod of approval. Years ago he'd been elected alderman in a huge landslide, and then quit four years later to open the bar. One of the few provably honest politicians in the city, he quit to keep his integrity. Most candidates walked away from his bar unendorsed and disappointed. The few upon whom he conferred approval cherished the moment. John Chester hadn't backed a loser in fifteen years.

Paul leaned back in his chair and enjoyed the air-conditioned murk. His head rested against the wall behind him. The front two legs of his chair hovered three inches off the floor.

44

He watched Ian Hume stride through the front door of Chester's bar. Exterior light briefly lit up the gloom. Ian didn't look to the back where Paul sat. John Chester had Ian's draft Heineken half poured before the reporter perched on a bar stool. They exchanged pleasantries about the value of air conditioning until Ian spotted Turner and walked over.

Ian turned a chair around and straddled it, leaning his elbows on the top edges and taking several long, satisfying drinks from his stein.

Ian Hume was the star reporter for the city's major gay newspaper, the *Gay Tribune*. Two years ago he'd won the Pulitzer Prize for investigative journalism for his exposé of the medical establishment's price-fixing of AIDS drugs.

Turner and Hume had gone through the police academy together and had been assigned the same district as beat cops. They'd come to respect and like each other. But Ian had gotten fed up with the system, and in addition made the decision to come out sexually. He'd gone back to school for his journalism degree and begun writing newspaper articles; then he'd quit the department to work full-time as a reporter for the local gay newspaper. Ian had been a great help to Paul in the emotionally difficult time after his wife's death, when Jeff was born. They had been lovers for three years and close friends since their breakup. Occasionally they had been of some help to each other on cases. Sometimes the sharing of information proved very helpful.

Ian belched obnoxiously and slammed his stein down on the table. He glared at John Chester. Turner watched the tall, broad-shouldered owner unhurriedly bring over a refill. He plunked the beer down, gave Ian a good-natured pat on the shoulder, and returned to his post behind the bar.

"Bad day?" Paul asked.

Ian shifted his six-foot-six frame so that his legs rested on a chair at the next table. He scratched his blond beard with both hands, flipped the slouch fedora he always wore into the middle of the table.

"Everything is fucking nuts at the paper. Nobody knows

how to handle this murder today. We hate Mucklewrath so much, and it's great to see him miserable, but to kill somebody's kid? You've got be totally nuts. I want to see the man chained, tortured, and exiled to another planet simply because he's such an ignorant fuck. Add his antigay stuff and I think he should be shot. Whoever offed him would be doing all of us a big favor, but you don't kill his kid." Ian shook his head. "I draw the line at that kind of shit."

"I got to be among the first on my block to hear the press release." Turner described the scene in the suite.

"I attended the press conference," Ian said. "It was more of the same shit. I can't wait for the day when a politician getting elected by bashing gays goes completely out of date."

"It worked for him once."

"It won't again, I hope. He's got united opposition in California this time." Ian took a long swallow of beer. "So, you got the case? Figures. You're good at this shit. It's got to be somebody getting revenge on the old bastard."

"You think so?"

"Don't you? I heard a radio report that the killers said, 'Sorry now, aren't you,' then killed her. That sounds like vengeance to me."

Turner shrugged. "The man had a lot of enemies."

"You could line up every liberal and minority-group member in the country and have a hard time narrowing down the list of suspects." Ian sipped from his stein for a minute, then said, "You know this isn't the first 'Sorry now' incident."

"Huh?" Turner said.

Ian drank, wiped his mouth with the back of his hand, and said, "Yep, it was in the *Tribune*, maybe even the *Sun-Times*. A notoriously homophobic legislator from Kankakee, a woman who opposed every gay-rights bill, every AIDS-funding bill, every women's-rights bill. She looks like a pig-faced cow."

"That sounds prejudiced," Turner said.

"I don't care. She voted against anything that might have benefited gay people in the remotest way."

"And probably every bill for every other minority," Paul said.

"Maybe so, but the point is the 'Sorry now' shit." Ian explained that the woman was inordinately proud of owning the oldest mansion in Kankakee and that it had been in her family for nearly a century. "Somebody torched it while she and her husband were on vacation. They lost everything. Priceless antiques, family heirlooms from England brought over before the American Revolution. They lost irreplaceable millions. Painted in bright yellow letters on the driveway was the message 'Sorry now, aren't you?'"

"Maybe I'll give Kankakee a call," Turner said. They had few other leads. He'd give it a try.

The sound level on the large-screen TV over the bar rose. They looked over. John Chester had turned on the Mucklewrath religious cable-TV station. They were broadcasting live from Soldier Field. The reverend was still talking about the murder. Tears streamed down his face as he described the scene that morning. Paul began to say something to Ian, but the reporter held up his hand. "Wait, I want to hear this."

Paul listened. On the screen the tears stopped. Minutes later the Reverend Mucklewrath was into full fury. Spectacular rages and mighty diatribes were the warp and woof of his religious tapestry. Now he was after the Chicago police. For not doing enough. For not assigning enough men. For not returning his phone calls. His voice rose to a screech as he called down God's wrath on those who failed in the investigation.

"Turn that shit down," Ian bellowed. John shook his head at the television set and slowly complied.

Ian grinned at Paul. "Well, you're in deep shit. The good reverend will have your ass in hell if you screw this up."

"It'll be a proper investigation, no matter if God intervenes or not," Paul said.

Ian took several healthy gulps from his stein of beer. "You set for tomorrow night?" he asked.

Paul sighed. "I rented the goddamn tux. I haven't worn one

since I went to the prom with Sheila Franzini eighteen years ago."

"Sheila Franzini?"

"She married a rich Italian baker's son, who is now, I believe, selling real estate in Hawaii, or Nome, or someplace."

"You'll have a good time tomorrow night."

"I've never gone to a 'bachelor auction' cruise on Lake Michigan."

Half the do-good groups in the city had discovered the benefit of having fund-raisers while cruising on Lake Michigan.

Turner took a gulp of beer and continued, "You, my son, and Mrs. Talucci all want me to get married."

"Who did your son notice?"

"A guy at the local auto-parts store."

"How butch!"

"I'm only going tomorrow night because it's a good cause."

John switched the TV over the bar to the nine o'clock news. They watched the lead item, various reports on the death of Christina Mucklewrath with extensive coverage of the reverend's speech at Soldier Field.

"Bastard," Ian said. He tipped his beer stein upside down so John would see he needed more. Paul still nursed his first one. "You know," Ian said, "he isn't the only antigay bastard who's gotten it lately."

Paul raised an inquisitive eyebrow.

"You heard what happened at the dinner for Veronica Balushka."

"A lot of people got sick, something like that?"

"That's how the *Sun-Times* and *Tribune* reported it, but as an ace star reporter, I know what really happened, just as I know anything and everything there is to know about the gay community in Chicago."

Turner ignored the boast and asked, "Are we talking murder here?"

"Nothing that dramatic. There was a brief item alluding to it in the gay papers. Did you see it?"

"No. I rarely pick up the gay papers. I've barely got the time to look at any newspaper. Plus you don't deliver."

Ian sighed. "I write brilliant news stories, witty columns, biting editorials, and wickedly funny movie reviews and you never see them."

"Did you want to tell me about Miss America or not?"

Ian said, "You remember the woman? Young, beautiful, curvaceous?"

"Aren't they all?"

"I suppose so. You did hear she resigned?"

"Yeah, the guys talked about it. Like Vanessa What's-Her-Name years ago."

"Right." The current Miss America, Veronica Balushka, had started a series of speaking tours in which she attacked gay people. The controllers of the pageant, wishing to keep their winner nonpolitical, insisted she stop. She wouldn't. She'd denounced them as closeted gays. Either voluntarily or having been forced to do so, she'd resigned a month ago and then began her latest tour, at times outdrawing the Reverend Mucklewrath. "Like you said, the newspapers reported that a lot of people got sick at a fund-raising dinner she hosted. I happen to know that people didn't 'get sick.'" Ian laughed. "They all got the runs."

"Huh?" Paul said.

"Diarrhea. The shits," Ian said.

"I didn't need a more graphic explanation. What I meant was, How does this connect with being antigay?"

"Rumor had it FUCK-EM was involved," Ian said.

FUCK-EM was a radical gay organization, fed up with the inability of other gay groups to change the world quickly enough to suit them. Turner knew they had a branch in Chicago. He also knew the acronym stood for nothing except the group's "in your face" attitude.

Ian took a swallow of his recently refilled beer and continued. "I tracked down the rumor to my usually impeccable sources. I can't prove it, but I'm sure it wasn't the food they served that caused the problem. I think one of the members of FUCK-EM got into the kitchen and put something into the food and gave them all the runs." Ian laughed.

"You didn't put that in the paper," Paul said.

"Nope. Couldn't prove it. It happened out in one of the suburbs—Schaumburg, I think. You should call the cops out there. See what they say."

"I can't imagine there being a connection," Turner said. "Or are you trying to say there's an international gay organization called the Queer Avengers, righting wrongs, protecting the weak, and doing good?"

"Make fun. It was exceptionally well planned. Only a limited number of people had access to the kitchen. No one claimed to see anything unusual. They haven't got a clue, certainly not a suspect."

"Normally, murderers—or any type of serial killers—don't branch out to other crimes. Some kind of pattern develops. There's no connecting method here," Turner said. "Besides, she must have lots of other enemies. We aren't the only ones who get singled out for attack by ignorant bigots."

"Do you have any clues in this one?" Ian asked.

"Right now it's the usual routine police work. Nothing promising at the moment."

They ordered another round of beers.

Paul tiptoed into Jeff's bedroom. It was after one. Brian had picked Jeff up from Mrs. Talucci's when he got home, as Paul knew he would. He felt very lucky to have a son like Brian who cared so much for his less-able brother.

Paul Turner had the normal anxieties any parent would about his teenage son. Did he try drugs? Would he be able to resist the peer pressure to do stupid things? Would he get drunk one night and end up smashed to pieces on an expressway. Was he trying sex? Was he being careful?

Paul remembered the conversation he'd had with Brian about condoms two years ago. Brian had been fairly amused, had simply told his dad he knew what they were and knew where to get them, if and when he ever needed them.

Paul stayed out of his son's bedroom. He didn't want to know if there were porno magazines stashed in the bottom of the closet or condoms in the dresser drawer. When guests visited, he closed the door.

Jeff lay in bed peacefully, light from the street below drifted through the boy's window. From it Paul could see the scar revealed by the covers gathered below his son's back. He sighed wistfully. He'd never gotten over the stage of knowing if he had all the magic power in the universe, the first thing he would do was touch his son's back and cure him. He thought of Christina and then imagined anyone trying to hurt either of his sons. He knew he'd never let that happen. He sat on Jeff's bed. With the back of his hand, he caressed the soft skin of his sleeping son's face.

FOUR

Saturday morning Paul Turner woke up to the sound of his older son talking to a friend on the phone. He heard him laugh raucously and then lower his voice. Turner felt no breeze as he glanced out the window. None of the leaves on the old oaks moved the slightest. The heat of another cloyingly humid day surrounded him. One of these years he wanted to air-condition his place. He took a shower and dressed in faded jeans and a sleeveless T-shirt with the University of Illinois Chicago campus logo on the front.

He wanted to get the morning chores done as quickly as possible. He had agreed to meet Fenwick at one to requestion the reverend and try to pick up any details on the case. He might even give the Kankakee and the Schaumburg police a call to check on what Ian had told him the night before. First he had domestic chores to attend to.

He started a load of wash, supervised Brian as the trash got taken out, refereed a brief argument between the boys—Jeff wanted to wear one of Brian's rock-group T-shirts. Vacuuming, floor scrubbing, bathroom cleaning all got done amid various grumblings, not all of which came from the two younger members of the household.

Tranquillity finally reigning in the house, he and Brian walked out to the garage. Paul had helped Brian buy an old car. Brian had insisted on a used Trans Am, even though Paul had told him they'd spend most of their time fixing it. In the six months since they had bought it, they had spent most Saturday mornings in the garage fixing it or taking it to the local mechanic so he could work on it. Early on Paul had installed a heater in the garage so they could work on it through the winter. He guessed that if you totaled up the amount of time the car had run without a problem, it would probably add up to less than a full week.

An hour into the work Paul squirmed out from under the car, followed by his grease-encrusted son. "We've tried everything else. It's got to be the starter switch," Turner said.

Brian nodded. "Can we get it today? Can we get it put in before you have to go to work?"

"I don't remember saying you could use the car tonight."

"Dad, this is too important to tease about. Let's go to Vargas's now." He nudged his dad. "You'll get a chance to talk to Ben."

"Talking to Ben and him talking to me does not mean he is gay and wants a date."

"Dad, I know how he looks at you. Even *I* know he's interested."

Paul shot out a hand to grab his son. Brian wasn't quick enough to dodge away. They wrestled briefly, grinning at each other.

Finally Brian slipped away. Turner panted slightly, eyeing his son askance. "You're getting too big to wrestle with, and how come you know so much about who I need to date?"

"One, you're getting old, and two, I go on dates and you don't. It works pretty much the same with girls, Dad."

Paul smiled at his son. "I guess I remember."

"That was so long ago," Brian said.

"You want the car fixed or not?" Paul said.

Paul had told Brian about his sexual orientation when the boy was eight years old. He didn't think Brian understood it completely then, but he was glad he had told him at that age.

Early on he'd been able to resolve questions and confusions about a father who was different, and Paul's openness and honesty over this issue led the two of them to develop a closer relationship than most fathers and sons. He had told Jeff last year, and so far the results had been the same.

They walked the half block to Vargas's Auto Parts Store. The Saturday-morning crowd milled around the pumps in front, the service bays in back, and the parts counter in the middle. Ben Vargas smiled when he saw them, finished with a customer, and came over to talk.

Turner observed more closely than usual Vargas's body and mannerisms. They'd gone through grade school and high school together. He knew Ben had gone away to college and he'd heard he was living in California. His boyhood friend had returned several months ago, when old Mr. Vargas retired and left the business to his son.

Ben stood an inch or two taller than Paul. He wouldn't be called handsome, but some might call him rugged. His hair hung a trifle longer than was usual in the neighborhood. His white shirt clung to broad shoulders and tapered into a pair of faded jeans that Paul admitted he noticed every time he came in. He looked up from the crotch of them now and saw Ben's eyes on his.

They discussed auto parts, Brian's foolishness in buying the Trans Am, old Mr. Vargas, now living in Florida; all while Ben let his help wait on other customers. They promised to get together for a cup of coffee at some indeterminate time in the future. They made almost the same promise to each other every time they spoke.

At one that afternoon Turner made his way through the building humidity and ninety-degree temperature. Wilmer and his stench did not greet him at the station door. Maybe he took Saturdays off, Turner thought, though Wilmer always seemed to be around.

First he called Sam Franklin in the crime lab. Sam said, "They used a .38 double-action revolver with a silencer on the end. Standard-issue cop gun in this city, except for the last part. Took us three hours to find the bullet in the sand. Lucky it was in one piece. Not much else to tell you. Almost seems like a mob execution." They talked a while longer, but Franklin had little other information. Turner thanked him and hung up.

He called California to ask about Jason Thurmond. He tried the sergeant he talked to the day before, but Sergeant Dooley was not available. It took fifteen minutes' worth of transfers to get her home phone number. He had to repeat his name, rank, and reason for calling three times. He suspected that in that time someone called Chicago to check on his validity.

He called her home and the line was busy.

Fenwick came in as he finished the call. They forced their way through the humidity to the car and drove to the Oak Street Arms. They ran into an ethnic parade moving down Michigan Avenue. Even with the police trying to smooth their way through the streets it took twenty minutes for a five-minute trip.

Sweat drenched both of them as they entered the air-conditioned bliss of the hotel. Upstairs, Donald Mucklewrath said, "What do you want to see my father about?"

"We'll tell him that," Fenwick said.

"You'll tell me." The son stood between them and further access to the suite.

Turner sighed. Fenwick was good at this sort of thing. He mixed the right amount of menace and innocence as he said, "Fine, we'll get warrants, arrest you and the reverend as material witnesses, and talk to both of you down at the station. I'm sure we could notify the press on our way."

Johnson walked in at that moment carrying a sheaf of papers. Turner noted Johnson's ashen look, and the fact that the papers shook in hands that trembled.

Turner told him they needed to see the reverend.

Johnson's voice didn't rise above a whisper, "He's free."

"What's going on?" Donald asked.

"I told him the truth," Johnson said.

"About what?" the thirty-five-year-old son asked.

"Everything," Johnson said.

"Which way?" Fenwick asked Johnson.

The older man nodded toward a doorway on the left, from which he'd emerged moments earlier.

Donald followed Fenwick and Turner. In the room the Reverend Mucklewrath knelt at the side of his bed, his elbows resting on the coverlet. Mucklewrath wore a severe black suit and a tie to match. He gazed up at the three of them. Finally, his Old Testament visage fixed on Turner.

Turner said, "Reverend."

The man responded by rising slowly to his feet. Instead of turning to the police he pointed a gnarled finger at his son. "Get out." Turner thought he sounded like Charlton Heston doing his best God imitation.

Donald Mucklewrath said, "What's going on, Dad?"

"You knew, didn't you?" the reverend said. "Don't try to deny it. Johnson has told me all about himself, what you knew, and what you yourself are guilty of. Now, get out. I will deal with you later."

Donald swayed back and forth as if he might faint, opened and closed his mouth as if trying to speak.

Mrs. Mucklewrath hurried into the room. "I just talked to Johnson." She spotted the police and abruptly stopped speaking. She eyed them all coldly.

The reverend said to his wife, "I need to talk to Donald at a more appropriate time. Could you?"

She marched over to Donald and said to him in what Turner thought was a surprisingly gentle voice, "Come with me, please, Donald." They left.

Mucklewrath walked slowly to a cushioned chair next to the window. Fenwick and Turner followed him and sat on a small couch.

Turner watched his face carefully. He saw furrowed lines around the mouth, and eyes, red spots on the high cheekbones, and a gleam of sweat on the upper lip. The man breathed deeply for several minutes. He stared out the window toward the high-rise next door and spoke without turning to them.

"Yesterday morning I knew God was with me. He'd granted me all the happiness he could give to a human. A beautiful family, a loving wife, a calling that I find deeply satisfying, an organization committed to God's work."

He reached out and tapped the glass with his knuckles. "The Lord is testing me. I shouldn't wonder 'Why me?' He tests us all according to our ability to bear the weight of the world."

Turner asked, "Reverend Mucklewrath, where did you go late Thursday night and early Friday morning?"

Mucklewrath still didn't look at them. He said, "I have no need to answer that question. It has nothing to do with what happened to"—he paused, then finished—"to Chistina."

"We need to know, Reverend," Fenwick said.

"You think you do, but you don't," the minister said. He turned to them with a wan smile on his face. "I'm going to tell you a little story." He held up a hand to forestall any protests they might make. "In telling the story all of your questions will be answered."

He moved his chair so it faced the two of them. Backlit by the window light, his face in shade, the reverend placed his hands palm up on his legs and began to speak in a low voice.

"I imagine you think I'm a fraud like all these other television preachers. I'm sorry to disappoint you. I have no mistresses, no extramarital affairs. I have no involvement in drugs. The books of all my organizations are open to anyone's inspection. I'm different from all the other preachers. I believe, and I am not out to cheat those who believe. I do not live in a palace.

"Many of my fellow preachers hate me for my honesty and openness. Many are jealous of my success. Some have been trying to be elected to political office or to influence the process of legislation the way I have. They all failed. I have succeeded. Jealousy is an ugly thing.

"I have flaws. I trust the people around me to a fault. I believe as God has chosen me, so has he chosen them. I should pay more attention to those around me.

57

"That Dr. Johnson consorted with women not his wife distresses me. It seems my son conspired with him and even at times paid for the services of women. Beyond this, I now know my son used his position in the organization to extort enormous sums of money from people who believed in me. You can ask him later. It seems many people were willing to pay him because they thought he could influence me. None of this money went through my organization. You will need to check his personal accounts."

"You see how honest I'm being? My own son a liar and cheat. Perhaps he didn't do something strictly illegal, but what he did was morally reprehensible. I'm afraid he may have done more that Johnson didn't know about.

"I have other flaws. One of them is that I don't sleep well at night, especially when on a speaking tour. The Lord speaks to me at those times. I awake, dress, and leave. I thought my movements a secret. I was wrong. I go to the missions we have set up in each city for the poor and homeless. I go there to the tiny chapels that we build in each shelter. I go there and I pray. Afterward I help out as best I can. I also talk to the faithful on duty. I speak with those who, like myself, cannot sleep and have come to us for serenity. One time I delivered a baby. Sometimes I help wash up the dishes, pots, and pans from the suppers we give. I've done lice-infested laundry. I sweep. I do whatever needs to be done."

"We'll have to check with your mission here," Turner said quietly.

"Of course. I've had no time to call them to warn them, although I would hope they would speak honestly with you, no matter what."

"Your first wife said you hid a lot of money."

"The records of the divorce are open. You are welcome to hunt through them."

After talking to the reverend, they interviewed the shaken Donald, who smelled suspiciously like bourbon. An emotional basket case, he was unable to give them any useful information about himself or his father.

In the car Fenwick said, "The reverend is a hypocritical, lying bastard. The guy is a double fuck if I ever met one."

"I think he told us the truth," Turner said calmly.

Fenwick ignored the comment and said, "And the rest of the family is for shit."

"No doubt about that," Turner said, then added: "They don't seem to be exceptionally broken up about Chistina's death. Except the reverend."

"You believe he doesn't know what the killers meant when they said, 'Sorry now, aren't you?'"

Turner reflected a minute. "No, I don't think he knows, at least not consciously. He's caught up with God and his cause. If we could get him down to the human level, we could possibly get something. I doubt it."

They drove to the address the Reverend gave them. At the Mission of Eternal Salvation on west Madison Street, they found numerous workers eager to confirm the Reverend Mucklewrath's presence late Thursday and early Friday. As a check on the mission worker's story, they spent some time afterward finding the cop on the beat, who gave them the names of a few of the regulars at the mission. After a half-hour search, they found one of the homeless lounging on a bench outside the Chicago Police Academy on Jackson. His name was Daren Brudasinski. He claimed to have talked to the reverend around two in the morning when he entered the mission.

Fenwick said as they drove back to the station, "Maybe Mucklewrath told the truth. Maybe he really doesn't know and doesn't have anything to do with the murder."

"If he doesn't, then that crowd around him sure must know something," Turner said, "and they haven't told us shit. It sure feels like they're hiding something. I'm going to try California again. I want to know about the campaign manager and the other preachers around the country."

It was nearly four when they pulled up at the station. It had rained briefly while they were in the mission, but instead of washing the atmosphere clean with fresh cool air, it had added to the mugginess. Turner sat in his shirtsleeves and turned the fan on full blast.

At their desks, Roosevelt and Wilson were each interviewing a white male. From listening, Turner thought they might have finally arrested the men in a series of robberies that had plagued the near North Side. Two men had made a science of attacking people using outdoor banking machines from the Chicago River to Rogers Park.

Roosevelt passed by Fenwick's and Turner's desks on the way to the small kitchen—storage room they had.

"Finally catch the bank guys?" Fenwick asked.

"Yeah, they tried a place at Michigan and Ontario. They got caught in traffic and their car overheated," Roosevelt said. "I never thought I'd be grateful to one of the parades down Michigan Avenue for making my life easier."

By the time he came back a minute later carrying a can of grape soda, Turner was already on the phone to California. This time he caught Sergeant Dooley at home.

He asked about the campaign manager, Jason Thurmond.

She said, "A nice guy. Not hard to work with. Of the whole crowd he was the most accessible. It wasn't surprising he quit."

"A lot of bad feeling when he left?"

"Not against the reverend, or at least none that he mentioned. It was pretty well known that his beef was with Mrs. Mucklewrath and the son. For all their supposed expertise, they're really political amateurs. I think it drove him nuts, and the reverend believes in family and trusting them. I can't see Thurmond being angry enough to murder the kid, and I certainly can't see any other motivation."

That was one thing that was driving Turner nuts in the investigation. So far no one in the inner circle had a reason to murder Christina. The other problem was that outside the organization, there could be millions of Mucklewrath-haters and just plain nutcases who could have done it.

"How about other preachers out there? Do any of them have a special hate for Mucklewrath?" Turner asked Dooley.

"That's tougher. You'd have to be able to check nationwide.

Out here I don't remember anyone being especially nice or nasty. I think those guys are a pretty independent lot. One of them tried to get a national conference of preachers going, but then they had all those scandals and everybody bailed out."

Turner glanced at the time. Saturday at five o'clock. Nearly thirty-three hours since the murder and they didn't have a lot of clues.

Feeling a little foolish, Turner put in a call to Schaumburg. The guy who answered growled unpleasantly, but talked to him, barely checking his identification. In gruff, terse words he told Turner they didn't consider the case anything significant, beyond the obvious that some people ate something and got sick. Turner was inclined to agree. He got almost the same reaction from his call to Kankakee.

Fenwick brought over the lab paperwork. It didn't tell them any more than they already knew. The crime lab had found nothing—other than the bullet—to indicate who might have done the killing. Turner and Fenwick spent an hour going over the reports from the cops who'd interviewed the people in the high-rises facing Oak Street beach. They still had numerous callbacks to make, but so far they'd turned up zip. Not even a glimmer.

At seven they gave it up. Spending all of Saturday night in frustration wouldn't help. Block, the case sergeant on duty, came through and told them to go home.

At the admitting desk downstairs Charlie Grimwald motioned for Turner to join him. Grimwald said, "Did you hear the news?"

Turner shook his head. Normally Charlie liked to talk and usually Turner didn't mind giving him some time, but he was in a hurry.

Grimwald said, "They found an old guy in the river this afternoon near Roosevelt Road."

"Who was it?" Turner asked.

"They aren't sure, but from the description, I think it might have been Wilmer. They said they found some little toy cars in his pocket. You know, the metal kind they've got for kids."

Turner gaped at him.

"You okay?" Grimwald asked.

Turner mumbled a yeah and asked that Grimwald be sure to let him know when they got a positive identification and get him any other information. Turner told him he would call sometime on Sunday.

Paul planned to meet Ian at the ticket booth at the west end of Navy Pier. He'd parked near Olive Park and walked the half block over. Staring up at the expanse of Lake Point Towers, he adjusted his collar and bow tie for the hundredth time. Brian and Jeff had teased him about going out. Ian had been trying to get him attached. Turner felt: If it happened, fine. He'd dated some nice guys over the years, but none seriously in a long while. He wouldn't go out of his way, but he wouldn't reject somebody interesting out of hand. He had two boys to rear and a hectic job. Enough for anyone.

A hand brushed his arm. A throaty voice said, "Hello, handsome."

Paul turned to see his friend attired in a similar tuxedo, but with a Mickey Mouse–motif dress shirt and bow tie.

"I like the understated look," Paul said.

"People are looking at you, my friend. You are fresh meat. And you are gorgeous. You should have let me put you up for auction. You would have grabbed the highest bids of the night."

Paul found himself blushing for the first time since second grade, when Monica Planifar had accused him of trying to look under her dress. Sister Suzanne had made him stand up in front of the whole class and apologize.

"I'm not looking for a husband, and I don't want to be auctioned off," Paul said. "Why don't you have them bid on your more famous columns?"

"This is supposed to make money," Ian said. He took his friend's arm and propelled him through the gate and along the pier. "There's enough husband material out here for any man to find somebody. Even the most responsible parent in the city might find Mr. Right."

Numerous excursion boats and a few private yachts were berthed along the pier.

Their destination was the boat *Heart of Michigan*, the largest excursion boat in the harbor. It had four levels. The top, open to air, was the smallest. The second and third levels actually combined to surround a small stage on which were staged minor musical productions. From the third level one could walk onto an open space on the stern of the ship. The fourth level was completely enclosed. The interior of the second, third, and fourth levels contained tables, set for elegant dining in a cruise-ship motif.

They walked up a gangplank to be greeted by smiling young men saying "Welcome aboard" and giving out cards that gave them a number by which they would be recognized if they chose to bid on one of the bachelors. Mobs of elegantly dressed men thronged the interior of the second and third decks.

Paul Turner dated and spent enough time in gay bars to recognize the stares of interest he got. Comfortable with people he knew, yet relatively shy with strangers, he wasn't all that thrilled about telling someone what he did. Saying he was a cop could lead to inappropriate fantasies, or immediate huffy disinterest on the part of potential dates. Once in a while the newly acquainted became belligerent. One of the hazards of being a cop.

One of his wife Gail's secrets had been the ability to talk to a handsome athletic teenage boy and make him comfortable in social situations. He thought, at eighteen, that the sex part would grow as they got to know each other. He'd been woefully ignorant and had put down his lack of performance expertise to lack of experience, not lack of interest. As the years had passed he'd realized it had been the latter and not the former.

He and Ian squeezed to the bar and managed to grab a couple beers. They left the air-conditioned interior and made their way to the top deck. Here the cool lake made their formal tuxes less uncomfortable. The heat of the day was at least bearable.

A group of men stood arguing animatedly in the stern. Ian waved to them and walked forward. Paul followed. Five of them greeted Ian eagerly, demanding to know his opinion of the chances of electing a gay or lesbian candidate to the state legislature.

Ian introduced Paul. He caught most of their names, but remembered one. A man with golden hair, short on the sides but hanging to his collar in the back, stood slightly apart. Ian introduced him as Dr. George Manfred. Paul guessed him to be in his early thirties. He might have been five foot six or seven. Paul saw bright blue eyes and smooth, tanned skin. The doctor caught his look and smiled at him. Beautiful, even teeth.

The others switched topics to the Reverend Mucklewrath and the murder. The discussion became quite heated. Finally one of them, Paul thought he remembered his name as Tighe, said, "I wish they'd killed him. I feel sorry for the daughter, but that shit-for-brains hatemonger deserves everything rotten that could happen to him. They should have killed him." Most of the men nodded agreement.

One of the others said, "I can think of a whole list of other people who it'd be great to get rid of. Think of it. A world without homophobes."

Paul listened, not contributing. Fortunately Ian had not introduced him as a cop. He didn't want to have to listen to their pet theories if they found out he was assigned to solve the murder. He felt out of place at moments like this. Briefly, he wished he hadn't come. When he turned into them again, they'd gotten onto the topic of Chicago politics. He felt his elbow brushed gently. Dr. Manfred smiled up at him. Paul had noticed him standing on the other side of the circle, also not contributing to the conversation.

Minutes later Paul found himself at the railing, deep in conversation. He could never remember what George Manfred first said to him. After fifteen minutes he realized he hadn't been this comfortable since the first days with Gail. He found out George was thirty-two years old. Born in southern Illinois, he had gone to college and medical school, and then completed his residency at Chicago City Hospital. He now devoted his practice to people with AIDS, especially those gay men too poor to afford decent care.

The doctor didn't comment when Paul told him he was a cop. Turner found himself talking about his sons, his hopes and dreams for them, Jeff's being born with spina bifida, and Gail's death.

Manfred sympathized quietly, then asked, "Did she know you were gay?"

"I'm not sure *I* did. Being gay would have put an end to the marriage eventually, more because Gail had a right to be sexually fulfilled. I'd begun to doubt my sexuality before Gail's pregnancy with Jeff. Then when he was born with spina bifida, and she died . . ." He drew a deep breath, then continued. "I'd known Ian. He helped a lot. We became lovers. He's a good man. We broke up, but he's still my best friend."

The boat cruised south on the lake with the Chicago skyline on their right. Paul had never seen the city he grew up in so spectacularly displayed. The lights of the skyscrapers soared above the twirling mass of cars rushing along Lake Shore Drive. "It's so beautiful," he said, and felt like a little kid.

George put his arm on Paul's shoulder, let it linger. Eventually the doctor talked about his boyhood in a small town. He talked about trudging to a one-room schoolhouse that had only twenty-two other kids. He talked about isolation and feeling different. Manfred didn't hear the word "gay" until he was in his senior year of high school. He spoke of the relief of escape, of going to college and medical school in St. Louis. He mentioned how seldom he dated because of his intensive studies in school and his exhausting routine now.

Paul didn't know if he wanted a major involvement at this point in his life, but on first impression George Manfred was certainly someone he'd like to get to know.

As Ian and Paul walked down the gangway the reporter pumped him for information about George. "Is it a relationship? Are you going out with him? He's a great guy. He's got a phenomenal reputation in the community. He can step into any meeting of warring factions and in minutes he's got them working together. I've seen him step in between two hissing queens and restore calm almost instantly. He's got those dreamy good looks and a personality to die for. Are you in love?"

"We exchanged phone numbers," Paul said.

"That's absolutely boring," Ian said. "Are you going to call him?" he demanded.

"I don't know. Maybe. Let's see if he calls me."

"Paul, nowhere is it written that the other guy has to call you first. You could call him."

"I am a cop with two kids, one of whom requires more than a moderate amount of parental care."

Ian grabbed him, turned him around, and put his nose an inch away from Paul's. "I have heard you say that so many times. What bullshit! He's nice. He's good-looking. He's got a career. Rumor has it he's independently wealthy. What more do you want?"

Paul shrugged off Ian's grip. "I didn't say I wanted more. I didn't say I wouldn't call him. I don't notice you waltzing off with Mr. Right."

"At this point I'll settle for Mr. Fairly Adequate," Ian said.

On Sunday morning Paul took his two boys to Sunday mass. They walked the three blocks to St. Felicitas'. Paul thought it hypocritical of a gay man to attend any kind of religious services, the churches having abandoned gay people long before Paul thought God might have. But he felt it was right for his boys. A year or so ago Brian declared he wasn't going anymore. Paul told him that when he graduated from high school he could make a choice about church attendance. Until then he had to attend. Occasionally, if Jeff felt the walk would be too much, they would push him in a wheelchair. In rain or winter Paul drove them to mass.

He and Jeff spent the afternoon at Brian's baseball game. They sat in the stands in the shade of an ancient oak that had survived years of neighborhood abuse. Brian pitched and played first base for the St. Felicitas High School team. Paul couldn't often make his son's games, but he got to as many as he could.

Jeff's spina bifida meant that at birth his spinal cord and nerves protruded in a sac from his back, near the bottom of his spine. He was born with bladder and bowel dysfunction and paralysis of his legs. Paul felt, and the doctors concurred, that it was better for Jeff to be treated as much like a normal child as possible. It was too easy for a parent, in guilt or remorse, to pamper, spoil, or overprotect a kid. Paul had seen the results when he'd gone on field trips with Jeff's classes before Jeff had been mainstreamed into a regular classroom in second grade. Many of the kids acted out, put on a show, or simply grossly manipulated parents too befuddled to cope. Not spoiling Jeff had been hard at first. Feeling sorry and monumentally guilty overwhelmed many parents of these kids. Turner's own common sense, along with Mrs. Talucci's realism, had gotten him over that.

They'd been fortunate the past two years. Jeff had gone to the yearly doctor's appointments and been reported in good health. Paul was glad for this, but knew he had to be continually watchful. Children with spina bifida could require emergency hospitalization, especially if the shunt placed in their head to drain fluid became clogged or had other problems. No amount of checkups or parental watchfulness could prevent such an occurrence.

Paul was enjoying the game and watching Brian run gracefully, in good health. He felt pride in Brian's natural ability. Having some of the same musculature as Brian enabled his younger son to master physical tasks far sooner than others with the same defect. Paul enjoyed sitting next to Jeff, observing the younger boy's adulation of his older brother and evident joy when Brian made a good play. Of course, Paul needed to take Jeff to the washroom so the boy could perform his ritual of urination. Jeff didn't complain, and Paul brought him back to the stands after the briefest of pauses. He talked to neighbors and friends. Kids stopped by to talk to Jeff.

Brian had permission to go out with his buddies after the

game, but since he had school the next day, he had to be in by eight to study for his final exams next week. Turner called the station when he got in from the game to see if there had been any developments in the Mucklewrath case. Nothing. He asked about Wilmer, but Wilson and Roosevelt, who had the case, weren't in.

Paul spent the evening playing checkers with Jeff and reading with him. He even found some time to work on household tasks that got put off too often. He managed to rebolt the handholds in Jeff's bathroom in less than an hour.

The phone rang at nine. Paul found himself wishing it would be George Manfred. Instead a voice he didn't recognize said, "We're watching you, cop. You'd make a good target on the beach, and your kids an even better one."

F I V E

Five minutes after roll call ended that morning Carruthers rushed into the squad room and ran over to Turner and Fenwick. "Lieutenant wants to see you," he said. "Are you guys in trouble?"

Turner said, "We'll have to see."

Carruthers said, "I watched all the newscasts last night. They all had a story about the murder. Snotty reporters asking stupid questions. I heard there's pressure from the Mayor's office to get this solved quick. Do you think it's part of a gay conspiracy, like the reverend said in his press conference?"

Fenwick gave him a sour look and marched to the coffeepot. He growled, "You watch too much TV news, and since when did you and the mayor become good buddies?"

In general Turner didn't mind reporters. He suspected this was Ian's influence. Carruthers tended to exaggerate most everything anyway.

Minutes later the two men walked into the lieutenant's office. They sat on two red vinyl-covered straightback chairs. From years of familiarity they ignored the stuffing protruding from the cracks in the seat covers. The lieutenant's desk and two large folding tables against the side walls nearly filled the room. The table on the left side contained neat stacks of files and forms; the table on the right had a recent-hurricane look because of the papers heaped on it. The lieutenant's desk had a phone, a picture of his family, several open folders, a pen set, and the lieutenant's elbows. He cupped his hands around his chin.

"Hell of a day," was his first comment. Outside a placid blue sky hid the fact that the weatherman had issued severe storm warnings until six that evening, with tornado watches and warnings possible. The only evidence now was a rising wind gusting to forty miles an hour.

The lieutenant picked a pen up and tapped it on the desk top. "What have you got on the Mucklewrath investigation?"

"Nothing," Fenwick said.

Turner filled the lieutenant in on what they had done and found out.

"Nothing," Fenwick said at the end.

The lieutenant scrunched his eyebrows together and pursed his lips. "What are you planning to do today?"

"Check any other lab reports, try to get a lead on other preachers. And I want to talk to Wilson and Roosevelt about Wilmer's death."

"The old guy died?" the lieutenant said.

"Yes. They found him in the river on Saturday afternoon. He claimed he knew who killed the little girl," Turner said.

"Did he?" the lieutenant said.

"Did he ever know anything?" said Fenwick. "I'm surprised he hadn't gotten around to confessing to this one."

Wilmer did have a habit of confessing to some of their more difficult cases. How he learned about them no one was sure. He hung around the station so much, Turner thought maybe he found out by osmosis.

"We haven't got much else," Turner said. "I think it's worth checking."

The lieutenant nodded. "Do it, although I'm afraid it won't lead to anything. Check the preachers. Go back over some of the same ground. The reverend has been making quite a stink in his speeches. The press hasn't gone totally nuts with this thing

70

because a lot of them don't like these preachers. We've been lucky so far."

"Do we have a political or press pressure problem?" Fenwick asked.

"I'll bet you can't say that again without screwing it up," Turner said.

The lieutenant said, "We'll worry about the press and politicians if we have to. For now, no."

At the door Turner turned back and said, "I got a call last night. Somebody threatened my kids. They mentioned the murder."

"You got a tap on the phone set up?"

"It's the first thing I'm going to do," Turner said. "The voice wasn't familiar. It might be nothing, but it's too suspicious and coincidental. I also called the Twelfth District. They'll put a special watch on, but they can't spare a twenty-four-hour guard. I warned the boys. Jeff gets help from my front door to school, and Brian promised to be extra careful. I told Mrs. Talucci this morning. She watches the kids after school. The whole neighborhood will be alerted before noon today. That'll help."

Fenwick asked him about the call as they sat down at their desks. He'd been to Turner's home numerous times and the families got together at least twice a year, at Christmas and for a summer picnic every July. "These people have to be fucking nuts," Fenwick concluded.

After a brief discussion Turner made the calls to set up the phone tap.

They decided to phone the police departments on the basis of Dooley's information from the day before. She had given them basic data on prominent televangelists not only in California but around the country as well. During the calls they got some sympathy because people recognized desperation tactics when they saw them. Many of them had been in the same position. Sympathy but little help. No one knew of any feuds of major proportions. One cop in Atlanta told Turner, "These guys are always squabbling about one thing or another. No one notices anymore."

After an hour and a half of futility they reached the end of their list.

"I'm open to any suggestions you've got before we try Wilmer," Turner said to Fenwick.

Buck got himself another cup of coffee and grumbled an okay. They walked over to Roosevelt and Wilson.

Turner explained to the two detectives what they wanted and why. Roosevelt and Wilson were happy to oblige. "A passerby saw something in the water and called the police. We got the call at"—Wilson checked some papers—"at four sixteen yesterday afternoon. They fished the body out from under the Halsted Street bridge. We assumed he got drunk and fell in."

"I wonder," Turner said. "I never knew Wilmer to be falling down drunk at that time of the day. That doesn't seem right."

"Could be any number of reasons," Wilson said. "Maybe he got in a fight with a buddy over a bottle, or he took a wrong step and that was it."

"Maybe he was pushed," Turner said.

"We'll get the autopsy report later today," Wilson said.

"The area canvassed yet?" Turner asked.

"Everybody who was around on Saturday was talked to. No one saw anything. We weren't planning to go back today. We didn't think it was important," Roosevelt said.

"It probably isn't," Turner said. "You don't mind if we go ask around?"

They didn't. They had plenty of other cases to work on.

On the Halsted Street bridge Turner glanced at the green Chicago River below. From here, it stretched a couple of hundred yards east, then curved north. Turner said to Fenwick, "Maybe he didn't fall off this bridge. Maybe he floated downstream. If we each took a side of the river and walked toward the Loop, we could talk to people and see if anybody knew anything."

Fenwick said, "Might as well give it a shot."

On his way to a rundown three-story fake tile-brick building, Turner walked under the shadow of the Dan Ryan Expressway. He glanced up at the concrete, saw the massive traffic tie-up typical for Chicago expressways during summer patching and reconstruction.

He talked to mechanics at marinas, and security guards at nearly abandoned warehouses, got snapped at by mean-looking German shepherds behind chain-link fences, and discovered nothing. He built up an itchy sweat in the close quarters of the old buildings, most of them un-air-conditioned and steaming.

After over an hour of plodding, and even getting lost once under the girders of the Dan Ryan Expressway, he came up with nothing. Wearily he trudged back to where they had left the car on Halsted Street. Fenwick wasn't in sight. Turner leaned on the railing, staring down at the water.

The flashing lights of an emergency tow truck caught his eye from the expressway he'd passed under several times. He watched the truck as it weaved through the snarled traffic. The waving yellow lights halted for a few minutes, then he saw the front half of a car begin to rise. Moments later they left. Turner kept his gaze fixed on the workers. They repaired expressways in Chicago all summer long, it seemed. To avoid tying up rush-hour traffic they especially concentrated on doing the work during midday, late in the evening, mornings, or on the weekends. They might have seen something if they were there last Saturday.

Fenwick trudged up a few minutes later. In the car Turner explained his idea.

They entered the expressway at Roosevelt Road and immediately found themselves in the traffic jam caused by the construction. It took twenty minutes to traverse the half mile to the workers. They pulled onto the far side of the barricades and got out of the car. First Turner took a long look around. He'd never walked on an expressway before and this portion of the Dan Ryan was elevated, so nothing blocked his view to the northeast, of the buildings of the Loop. Due east he saw railroad yards; to the west he could see the houses of the Pilsen neighborhood just south of his own. Directly north and south, snarled traffic fought its way through the midday construction.

They talked to the manager of the work crew. The same guys

who had worked Saturday afternoon making overtime were at work now. The manager took them to each man in turn. Most, like the manager, wore heavy work boots with thick socks, jeans, T-shirts, and hard hats. A few of the younger men wore cutoffs and no top. Deeply bronzed parts of exposed flesh glinted in the sunlight.

They strolled around freshly poured squares of cement and mounds of jagged pieces of rock. Past one spot where the concrete had yet to be poured, Turner could see the exposed cables and girders. Once he thought he caught a glimpse of street far below.

They talked to clumps of men. No one had heard or seen a thing. The manager felt it necessary to apologize after they talked to the last group.

"Is that everybody who was here?" Fenwick asked the manager in front of the last group.

"I think so," the manager said. His name was Arnold Fleckstein. Muscles like cannonballs bulged along his arms and shoulders.

A gray-haired man in his sixties said, "Billy's in the john. He was here."

The tiny group looked toward the portable john. The door opened and a slender, broad-shouldered, blond man in his late teens or early twenties stepped out. He noted the gaze of the crowd and strode over. Portions of his white jockey shorts peeked out at the belt and crotch of skimpy cutoffs. Without a shirt, he presented a well-tanned hairless chest for admiration. He smiled easily at the cops and spoke in a soft voice when he said hello.

Fenwick asked him if he'd seen anything on Saturday.

"I think maybe I did. I drink so much water that I can't sweat it all away. I'm always going to the john to piss." He scratched his left ear, then said, "I don't know though."

Turner and Fenwick took the man aside. He told them his name was Spike Bergenson. On Saturday he'd gone to the john as he said. He'd had to wait a minute for somebody already inside.

7 4

Bergenson said, "I looked over on the south bank there and saw three guys. I guess I wouldn't have noticed them except they wore kind of dark, heavy clothes, didn't fit the weather. They looked out of place, you know, suspicious."

"What did they do?" Turner asked.

"Nothing much. They kind of watched the water for a while then drifted off past the boats. I couldn't have seen them for sure more than half a minute."

"Did they look in a hurry or scared? Did they stare around them?" Turner asked.

"Not really. They just looked like guys hanging around."

"You didn't see where they went?" Fenwick asked.

"Nah. The guy came out of the john so I went in. It pays to hurry around here. Old Arnold don't like it when he thinks you're loafing."

"Did you see anything in the water?" Turner asked.

"Like what?"

"Anything."

"A couple little boats. Nothing unusual. What should I have seen?"

"Maybe a dead body," Fenwick said.

The kid gulped and said, "Oh."

Turner and Fenwick walked to the portable john and peered over the edge where the kid must have looked on Saturday. He wouldn't necessarily have seen anything in the water from this height. It was a little surprising he'd even noted the men.

"It was the same guys," Fenwick said.

Turner agreed then added, "And they've got to be amateurs. I want to check out Gangs and Narcotics when we get back just in case. I'd bet these three are acting on their own. Nobody who's a pro threatens a cop or his family. Too much unnecessary heat."

"Unless you busted somebody recently who's big in the gangs," Fenwick said.

"We've busted the same guys for the past two months, and we've worked on the other cases together, even if we arrested them on our own. Nobody anywhere mentioned connections.

We usually get a call from somebody at either Gangs or Narcotics if we have something more than we know."

"Okay, we're clean the last few months," Fenwick said. "It doesn't mean it couldn't be somebody from the past. Remember that woman who said she'd get you for arresting her for beating her husband."

"Tell me you really believe she's behind all this," Turner said.

"I'm just suggesting, is all," Fenwick said.

"Let's get back so we can do some checking."

Back at the station he had a message from Ian to call. He tried the *Gay Tribune* office, but Ian was out. While Fenwick called a friend who worked with Gangs. Turner called Organized Crime. They had no hints for him about anybody angry enough to threaten cops.

Fenwick reported on the talk he had with the Gang Crime Unit. "Nothing. Nobody's noticed any unusual activity of any kind. The guy I talked to said he'd put out a couple of feelers, and he'd do some checking with our guys who have mob connections."

Turner called Narcotics. After he hung up from them, he told Fenwick, "Same thing. No unusual activity, and he'd put out the word, same as Organized Crime."

Charlie Grimwald, the old officer on the desk downstairs who occasionally drove a squadrol on busy nights, came upstairs with their lunches. He'd caught them on their way in to ask if they wanted anything. Turner had ordered Italian beef with hot peppers from Angel's Coffee Wagon.

Charlie Grimwald delivered Turner's sandwich, collected his money, and then leaned down close. Turner got an up-front view of the white hairs sprouting from the old man's nostrils. Charlie put his hand on Turner's shoulder and whispered. "If anything happens to your kids, that guy is dead meat. You know we'll be watching in case somebody tries, but people are crazy." He squeezed Turner's shoulder tightly and repeated, "If anything happens, the killer dies. It may only be vengeance, but it will be something."

Turner watched the old man's eyes. He saw drops near the

corners. Charlie suddenly straightened up, snuffled loudly, rubbed his hand vigorously over his nose, and shuffled away. Turner knew word of the threat had spread among his colleagues. He knew the sincerity of promises made by men like Charlie Grimwald. At the annual station picnic every summer in Lincoln Park he'd seen Charlie push Jeff's wheelchair to various zoo exhibits, and pick him up to bring him closer to the animals. Jeff didn't trust a lot of people to carry him, but the beefy old cop was one of his favorites. For the moment, though, Turner wanted to concentrate on preventing an attack on his kids.

Turner started his lunch. Halfway through his sandwich Ian called.

"Did you call the good doctor?" was Ian's first question.

"I've been a little busy," Turner told him.

"Get a break in the Mucklewrath case?" Ian asked quickly.

"Nope. What'd you call about?"

Ian ignored his question and said, "I hear the good doctor is going to be at a party tonight. You should go. You should call him. Don't wait for him to call you."

Turner sighed, then said, "Ian, we're busy. Do you have something for me besides gossip?"

"Promise you'll go to the party tonight and I'll tell."

"I'll try to make it. Now what?"

"I assume that's the best promise I'll get out of you, and what I've got is another homophobic bastard getting it."

Turner said, "I've tracked down the other two incidents you've given me. There is absolutely no connection I can find between the them. I can't find a glimmer of a hint that either of those is connected to the murder. Start with major problem one. There is no way the killers could have known that Mucklewrath and his daughter would be on that beach at that time."

Ian started to speak.

Turner interrupted. "Think about it. They couldn't have. They had to be waiting for the opportunity. They needed him there with his daughter. Arson and mass diarrhea are well planned and well thought out, but they are not the usual crimes we connect with someone who goes on to be a killer. It just doesn't work."

"Do you want to listen or not?" Ian asked.

"Okay," Turner gave a resigned sigh.

"You know Jay Kendall, the columnist?"

Turner grunted a yes. Jay Kendall wrote a syndicated column, based in Chicago. A couple of years ago he had achieved the coup of a lifetime when both the *Sun-Times* and the *Tribune* started carrying his column.

"You know he owns all those racehorses in Kentucky?"

Turner tapped a pencil on his desk. "Somebody cut off a horse's head and put it in his bed so he'd see it when he woke up. I saw *The Godfather* twice, Ian. So he crossed somebody in the gambling world or the mob."

Ian resumed as if he hadn't been interrupted. "He attacks gays in his column in a mean-spirited, vicious way. He held a news conference this afternoon. He's prided himself all these years on always telling his readers the truth. Remember the series he did on legislators in Springfield, and their amorous involvements while in our beloved state capitol?"

"Yeah, he refused to name names for some reason. Supposedly his source took him to an expensive bordello. Some madam gave him hot inside information."

"You got it. Only he claimed he was saving the names for the next election."

"So."

"It was all a setup, all fake."

"Huh?"

"You heard me. He called the news conference to apologize. He's furious. He's determined to find out who set him up."

"Any idea who did it?" Turner asked.

"I've got my suspicions."

"The international gay conspiracy? Even if it was, as far as I can tell, whoever set him up didn't do anything illegal. If they actually gave him names, that could be some problem, I suppose. I just think it's funny. Somebody finally made a fool of him after he's done that all these years to other people. He had lots of people who hated him."

"Yeah. Half the cops in the state for a start. He opposed giving cops raises unless the crime rate went down. The guy has criticized almost everybody from the governor on down to homeless bums on the street. Not that the governor couldn't use getting his butt chewed out once in a while, but you know what I mean."

"How'd he find out it was a setup?"

"They sent him a note explaining the whole operation. They didn't sign it, but they did end it 'Sorry now, aren't you?'"

Off the phone, Turner filled Fenwick in. "What I don't get is the "Sorry now' shit. Okay, if it's revenge, but why not say who you are so the victim knows why they're suffering." Turner shook his head. "They've got to be coincidences, but more important, these other things aren't murders."

Fenwick thought a minute. "If any more happen, we can follow them up, but I wouldn't put much stock in them."

Turner called the medical examiner's office. They put him through to the M.E. in charge of Wilmer's autopsy. He'd talked to Gerald Miller numerous times, but they'd never met. Miller's high, tinny voice led Turner to picture a grossly overweight man in his late fifties, pale and effeminate. In actuality Miller was five foot three and twenty-eight years old, and weighed 130 pounds.

Turner asked about Wilmer's autopsy. They hadn't gotten to it yet. Miller asked, "He's more than just a bum off the street?"

"Maybe. I'm not sure. When you do the autopsy, could you check for anything suspicious?"

"Come on, Paul, I can check for years for suspicious stuff. We always check for something suspicious. How long you been doing this? I need something a little more specific."

Feeling slightly stupid, Turner thought a minute. "Start with blows to the head. If he hit his head as he fell, I guess it wouldn't prove anything, but check it out. Then maybe any kinds of poisons—and, oh yeah, as many blood tests as you can."

"You got it," Miller said, and hung up.

Turner sipped some coffee, saw the commander striding across the office area. The Chicago Police Department was probably unique in having the office of commander. It came about because of a scandal in the police department in the 1960s. The new police commissioner wanted reform, but the entrenched captains, then the rulers of the police districts, were nearly untouchable. At the time the police districts' boundaries matched those of the political wards. Politicians and cops, it was suspected but rarely proved, lived in a snugly symbiotic relationship unreceptive to alterations in their all-too-often lucrative practices. The new commissioner simply put a new person in command of the district and placed the formerly autonomous captains in sets of two, three, or four in redrawn districts. Now they had someone to report to who was directly connected to the commissioner's office instead of a politician.

The commander, a tall black man, sat on the corner of Fenwick's desk nearest the coffee machine. Turner liked the guy. He spent a lot of his time boosting the egos of men and women who usually met only the dregs of society at their worst. Cops face burnout, discouragement at the monumentality of their task, and awareness of the inherent futility of their jobs. They can't eradicate crime and stupidity, but spend eight hours every day trying to do just that. The commander worked as many hours as the detectives, kept out of their way, and respected their professionalism.

In his soft raspy voice he asked about their progress in the Mucklewrath case. Turner explained what they'd done and what their conclusions were so far.

The commander nodded carefully at the end and said, "You're doing fine, but we've got all this bullshit from the press, politicians, and preachers. I'll hold them off for as long as I can." He wished them luck and strode out.

"We do have a motive though," Turner said. "Whoever it is wanted Mucklewrath to be sorry that his daughter is dead. Who would want him to suffer that much?"

Fenwick asked, "Who has he hurt who would think the murder of his daughter is equal to the suffering they've had?"

They shrugged their shoulders. Neither had an answer to the other's question.

They spent much of the afternoon checking the reports on the callbacks the beat cops had made to people not home on their first canvass. Turner and Fenwick followed up on a few of them who still hadn't been home. They came up with a total of nothing. They spent the latter part of the afternoon and the early evening filling in forms.

By eight they looked at hours more work. Turner, jacket off, tie loosened, shirt unbuttoned, and three cans of diet soda empty on his desk, stood and stretched. "I can't believe this shit," he opined unhappily.

The light on his phone for the internal extension blinked. He eased it out of its cradle and rested it on his shoulder. "Yeah," he said.

"Somebody to see you, Paul," said the desk sergeant from downstairs.

"This person got a name?" Turner rubbed his eyes with his left hand.

Silence a moment. "A press guy. Want me to get rid of him? Says his name is Ian something."

"I'll see him." But at the moment Turner didn't want to go to a party.

Ian had visited the squad room a few times before. He nodded to Fenwick.

Turner said, "I don't have time for a party tonight."

"I have news, but yes you do."

Turner plunked himself onto his swivel chair and put his feet up on the desk. Ian sat in the suspect chair. Fenwick placed his elbows on his desk and leaned closer.

Ian addressed the two men. "We got another one."

Turner sat up a little straighter.

Ian held up a picture. The two cops squinted at the 8½-x-11 piece of paper.

Turner said, "It's some naked guy in bed with a woman. This is news?"

"Not a very good picture," Fenwick said. "It'll never sell as pornography. She's too ugly and he's too old."

"You don't know who he is?" Ian demanded.

The cops stared harder at the picture, then looked up at Ian and shook their heads. Turner said, "But you're going to tell us, aren't you?"

"Every paper in town got this a little over an hour ago along with an anonymous note. This is Ted Saimont, auxiliary bishop in the Archdiocese of Chicago. It doesn't say who she is. Besides rebuking the bishop for his transgressions against humanity, it ends with the words 'Sorry now, aren't you?' No one at the chancery office, including the bishop, has been available for comment."

Turner said, "Who would do this?"

Ian said, "Everybody. The guy led the campaign to close down abortion clinics. He made himself a general pain in the ass to every liberal cause. He got in trouble with the pope because of his push to have the Catholic mass done in Latin again."

"This doesn't help," Fenwick said.

"If it's a conspiracy—" Ian began.

"Which I don't buy," Turner said.

Ian went on imperturbably, "If it's a conspiracy, these people have ways of finding out and operating on a fairly sophisticated level. They could do murder."

Turner read the note attached to the picture. "It says this is what he gets for hurting the innocent. I'd like to know a little more about this."

"Good luck getting through the church stonewall."

"Anybody going to print the pictures or story?"

"I doubt it," Ian said. "It's embarrassing and amusing, but it arrived anonymously. Even we at the *Gay Tribune* have journalistic standards. We aren't some sensationalist tabloid."

Turner said, "I'll try and talk to the columnist Jay Kendall and to this bishop tomorrow. I still don't buy this conspiracy crap."

"Double fuck," Fenwick said. "Let's go home and start fresh in the morning."

Outside, Turner and Hume leaned against Paul's car. Ian said, "I finally got to hear the famous Fenwick say 'double fuck.' I think that in itself makes this trip worthwhile."

Turner opened his car door.

Hume said, "This bishop gave antigay speeches all over the country."

Turner said, "I promised I'd look into it."

"You have to come to the party."

"Are you nuts? I've got to work tomorrow. The paper on this case stretches from here to Peoria. Give it a rest."

"The good doctor, George Manfred, will be there."

Turner stopped himself getting in the car. "That's dirty pool."

"I know he'd love to see you."

"Who says?"

"I just know."

"I've got to get home to my kids."

"I took the liberty of renewing my acquaintance with Mrs. Talucci before I stopped over. She has the situation well in hand. She said for you to go and have a good time."

Ian, the tall, vaguely aristocratic WASP, and the relentlessly ethnic Mrs. Talucci had gotten on famously from the first time they'd met.

"I'm going to check on the boys," Turner said.

"I took a cab over knowing you'd be reasonable, so you can drive."

"I'm not staying late, and if you don't have a ride, you can walk home."

"Agreed."

Paul found Brian at Mrs. Talucci's kitchen table studying for his advanced physics final exam. His son glanced up long enough to greet his dad and say, "Hi, Ian," before quickly returning to his papers.

They discovered Jeff and a friend playing Nintendo in Mrs.

Talucci's living room. She'd bought the set for Jeff two years ago. Paul watched for a few minutes as his son zapped various animated bad guys. At a break in the action he gave him a hug. Mrs. Talucci came down from upstairs to tell him to go and have a good time.

Gill Garret, a friend of Ian's, threw a party once a year for his own birthday. He lived in the top-floor apartment of a three-story brick building on Belmont Avenue a block west of Broadway. Tonight balloons crammed the apartment from front door to back. Turner noticed that most of the balloons contained words or phrases that had nothing to do with birthdays. Gill might have gone to a party caterer's and purchased ten of every kind they had.

Turner had met Garret several times before and liked him. After hellos, Ian remarked, "I love the balloons, but some of them don't seem to match the occasion."

Garret, a tall broad-shouldered man who worked in a steel mill, said, "I know. I thought it would be a kick to buy all of them. So I did. Don't you love it?"

Garret's lover, one Neil Orkofsky, whirled by with a tray of drinks in his hand and said, "It looks like shit, but it's better than last year."

Ian explained to Turner as they grabbed drinks and moved to a corner of the front room near the front door and next to a grand piano. "Last year's party he decided on a jungle motif with real plants and real rain. It took three days to clean the mess."

"I don't see the good doctor," Turner said.

"He'll be here. Gill promised me."

"You told him?"

"Paul, we're all interested in the cause of true love."

Turner guessed at least forty people must have been crowded into the apartment. Many greeted Ian with profuse enthusiasm. Ian introduced them to Paul, who caught most of their names. More than a few cast appreciative glances over the cop's body.

He'd worn faded jeans and a black T-shirt. With his five o'clock shadow he could have been a model for one of the more rugged men's colognes.

Turner sipped Budweiser from a can and wished he hadn't come. Ten minutes later he crushed his tin beer can, dropped it in a trash basket next to the piano, and prepared to leave. At the moment Ian's audience consisted of two extremely young and incredibly attractive men. He remembered their names as Rusty and Ernie. Briefly Turner wondered if they were over the age of jailbait, but discovered a second or two later that he didn't care. He waited for a pause in their conversation to say good night to Ian.

The two men Ian was talking to had dark short-cropped hair, wore tight jeans and gym shoes with no socks, and carried their shirts stuffed into the back pocket of their jeans. Rusty's vaguely red hair accounted for the unimaginative nickname his class-mates must have stuck him with in second grade. He sported a bruise above his left eye and spoke in a whine: "So the trick smacked me right in the bar. I told him if he wanted that kind of action, he'd have to pay more. The asshole didn't want to pay. I knew I shouldn't have started up with a drunk. Then that bull of a bartender, you know, the one with the droopy mustache and the mirrored earrings, down at the Womb?"

Paul didn't know or care.

The young man's voice rose several octaves. "The stupid shit called the cops. He didn't even tell us. It's not as if we haven't thrown some business his way. Well, the cops showed up, and they were just brutal. They demanded to know what we were up to. We told them we were there for a drink."

The other spoke up. "They couldn't prove anything. They were just being mean. They shoved us outside and made us put our hands against the car and everything."

The first said, "I wouldn't have minded being patted down, but they were two of the ugliest straight males I have ever seen. Fat asses from sitting in cop cars and devouring doughnuts. Why couldn't they leave us alone?"

At the end of the question Turner surprised himself by saying,

"Maybe they didn't leave you alone because you were doing something illegal. If you hadn't been selling yourself, there wouldn't have been a problem."

"Well, who's Mr. High and Mighty?" Rusty said.

Ian began, "Paul—"

Ernie interrupted him. "He's a cop. I can always spot them. I thought so when I walked in, but I can't resist a sexy ass in tight jeans. That almost got me busted two months ago." Abruptly his tone changed. "What are you doing at this party?"

Rusty turned on Paul and asked, "You a closet case come to check the opposition? Ian, how could you bring someone like this to Gill's party?"

"He's a friend, and there's no need to mouth off, Rusty," Ian said.

Ernie jumped in. "All cops are homophobic bastards." He spoke loud enough that they began to draw a crowd.

One thing cops tried to be careful about was who they socialized with, because of just such situations. At too many parties somebody with a grudge against a cop took the opportunity to complain about the transgressions of those who gave them tickets, or didn't respond quickly enough, or who had been brutal to a friend, or who had harassed the particular minority they might be a member of. Cops were so careful about being seen off-duty that they told rookies at the police academy never to drive to work in their uniforms. If you did, you were an open invitation to any nut, angry at any cop, who might take it out on you.

Rusty planted himself in front of Turner and jammed his finger into the cop's chest.

Ian tried to insert his body between them, but the muscular little whore shoved him out of the way, knocking off Ian's slouch fedora in the process. Turner didn't want to hurt the guy, wanted no trouble at all. He cursed Ian inwardly. Rusty began shouting, emphasizing the loudest words with continued jabs at Turner's chest.

At just that moment the door swung open and a commanding voice said, "What the hell is this?"

George Manfred strode into the room. Paul noticed that Rusty immediately stopped and looked sheepish. He remembered Ian's comment Saturday night about Manfred's reputation and ability to calm situations instantly. George gave Paul a friendly smile, then turned a withering stare on Rusty. "You're drunk. Go home. Where's Gill?"

Their host emerged from the back of the crowd. "I was in the john. What's happening? Hi, George, glad you could make it."

George said, "Rusty and Ernie need to be somewhere else in this universe."

To Paul's surprise the two hustlers complied quickly and meekly.

Minutes later, a new beer in hand, Paul, Ian, and George talked quietly in a corner.

"How did you do that?" Turner asked.

"They know me," the doctor said simply.

"George can't tell you, but I can," Ian said. "Six months ago Rusty had a bad scare about AIDS. He thought he had one of the opportunistic infections. Turned out to be an ordinary case of pneumonia."

"Not—?" Paul began.

"No, although I doubt if it's through any fault of his own that it wasn't," Ian said. "He lavished a lot of gratitude on George when he found out it wasn't AIDS. Trumpeted his virtues around the gay community for months." Ian frowned. "Strange thing is, Rusty's very bright. He got a Rhodes scholarship, but turned it down. Being sexy gave him a huge income with less work, I guess. Forget him. It's good to see you, George."

Minutes later Ian left them, and Manfred and Turner found a seat on a bench in a window bay. They sat letting their bodies touch at the shoulders, hips, and thighs. Paul enjoyed the closeness and warmth.

By midnight they'd promised to get together the next day if their schedules permitted. They lingered, arms holding each other tightly, sharing their first kiss on the landing just outside the apartment.

★ ★ ★

Ian teased Paul about the good-bye as Paul drove him home.

Turner asked, "How did he control those two so well? I'm a cop and supposed to be able to do it that quick. I just wanted to avoid a scene."

Ian said, "I told you. George Manfred is one of the most respected people in the gay community. Everybody, or at least everybody at Gill's party, knows of him. He's been with them when their friends have been dying. He's the most gentle and kind man. He'll spend huge amounts of time with grieving significant others. It's why he has no time. He needs to meet somebody just like you."

S I X

The next morning Paul gave Brian permission to go with his friends to the amusement park, Great America, after his exam. Brian's summer job with the Chicago Park District didn't start for a week, and this was his last final. But Jeff still had three days of school and the two boys squabbled over this disparity at breakfast until Paul had to declare a truce.

Paul found himself unaccountably smiling from time to time. Meeting Manfred again felt good. He'd definitely call him when he got a minute.

As Paul eased his way through rush hour, the weatherman confirmed the bright blue skies and seemed almost apologetic about the false tornado-watch alarm the previous day. The cold front had stalled for at least twenty-four hours at the Mississippi River. When it moved southeast, the weather in the entire state could get dangerous. The miserable early-morning temperature held in the low eighties, an unpleasant harbinger of sticky sweat all day.

No breeze disturbed the half-raised shades of the open windows of the squad room. Grumbling about the heat took up a large part of the conversation at roll call. Besides the usual Wednesday inspection of equipment, weapons, and ammunition, they endured the routine of current cases, reports that needed to be noted, who had to be reminded of court dates, crimes or criminals from the previous shifts they needed to be aware of, announcements of recent directives, lists of wanted persons and vehicles, and stolen-auto messages.

After roll call Block, the case sergeant, cornered Fenwick and Turner away from the others.

"We're getting a lot of pressure on this Mucklewrath daughter case. A lot. We've got to get something."

"We don't have anything," Fenwick said.

"Well, you better. Soon. I'm not risking my ass for some two-bit preacher's daughter. Find something, anything. At the least we've got to tell the press we've got some suspects."

Fenwick said, "We could round up the usual suspects."

Block said, "Don't get cute with me. Just get me some results." Block stalked off.

At their desks Fenwick muttered, "Double and triple fuck. What does that numbnuts think we're doing?"

Turner sighed. "If we even had a glimmer of a direction to go in, it would help. We knew this would get political. It's happened before. We'll ride it out."

"I wish we could get some kind of break," Fenwick said.

Then they began working on more paperwork. At ten Ian called.

"I just got an anonymous tip about Donald Mucklewrath," Ian said. "It's real strange. I'm not sure I believe it."

"What?" Turner asked.

"My source says that Donald is gay."

"And why is that significant?" Turner asked.

"Supposedly there's been a big fight about 'outing' him especially among gays in Chicago." "Outing" was the method some gay activists used to publicly identify closeted prominent gays and lesbians. One object was especially to make self-hating gay people less likely to do harm to their own. Another reason was to identify positive gay role models.

"I'm missing the connection to his sister's murder," Turner said.

90

"I'm getting to it. If he's gay, and if his sister found out, and if she threatened to tell her dad—"

Turner cut him off. "The evildoer turning out to be a closeted gay guy? Give me a break! You read too many cheap gay detective novels."

"But—" Ian began.

Turner interrupted again. "Besides which, that's an awful lot of ifs strung together, and the sister isn't around to confirm or deny any of the facts."

"Now can I talk?" Ian asked.

Turner grunted.

"I didn't say it was a good theory or even that I believed it. I just thought you might want to check it out."

Turner sighed. "I'm sorry. You're right. It's not much."

Ian said, "If Donald was under a strain because he's gay it could have caused or still be causing problems. You mentioned how strange and closed that group is. Here's your chance to break through and really learn something."

"Okay, okay. Where'd you find this out?"

"One of the guys here at the office, and he didn't remember where he heard it."

"Big help," Turner said.

Ian thought a minute. "I've got to check on who's who in the outing crowd, but you can start with Nate Robeson. He's a lawyer and head of the largest legit gay political organization in the city. Group is called Come Out for Freedom." Ian gave him details, said he knew the guy and would call to encourage him to be open when the cops came to talk.

Turner hung up and filled Fenwick in.

"I wanted something," Fenwick said, "but this is only a smidgen above nothing."

"I agree," Turner said, "but we've got nothing else. Anything that helps us understand the dynamics in that family might be helpful. So far we know very little about them."

"You're right. So Ian's setting up the meeting?" Fenwick asked.

"Said he'd call me back as soon as he found out anything."

While waiting for the call they turned back to their paper-work. Fifteen minutes later Fenwick said, "You know you're humming?"

Turner looked at him. "I am?"

"You are. You've been awful bright and cheery for a fairly fucked-up day. You met somebody. What's his name?"

"I didn't think it showed. His name is George, and to answer your other questions: He's a doctor, in his early thirties, he's nice, and I'm not in love."

"You'll have to bring him to the picnic next month," Fenwick said. "Madge and I will have to give our seal of approval."

"We only met a couple of nights ago," Turner said. "Let's not have wedding bells yet. He could be secretly married or be having an affair with Barbara Bush."

"It'll be good for you to get out," Fenwick said.

Years ago, at the annual Area Ten picnic, Madge Fenwick had introduced herself to Turner. They shared ideas on child rearing and on Buck, who'd become Turner's partner not that long before. At a moment when seven-year-old Brian was wheeling his brother around picnic tables, Madge said to Paul, "You're gay, aren't you?"

Paul said, "A homosexual with two kids."

Long after all the others left that day, the two families stayed and talked. The three adults sat under an oak tree and let the evening darkness gather around them. The smaller kids fell asleep on a nearby blanket. Brian played by himself on the baseball field, throwing the ball up, hitting it, then retrieving it, getting as many hits out of the bat as he could before the fall of night stopped him.

Madge had a nephew who was gay. Buck's attitude was that Paul was a good partner and a friend. Paul liked their down-to-earth good nature. They'd been friends since that day.

An hour later Ian called back. He'd set up an appointment for three o'clock. Robeson taught classes at Oliver Wendell Holmes Law School most of the day and wouldn't be free until then.

Fenwick and Turner grabbed a late lunch at a deli on the

corner of Dearborn and Congress, then walked over to their interview.

Oliver Wendell Holmes was a small law school located on six floors of a high-rise on State Street, a block north of police headquarters. The building contained old-fashioned elevators with manual controls. The elevator operator deposited them on the sixth floor after two tries at making the car floor level with the hallway.

Finding the office door with Robeson's name on it, they knocked. Seconds later a man in his early thirties, wearing a dark gray suit, answered.

Introductions over, they sat in the narrow office. Books lined the two longer walls. The window in the third wall, opposite the door, looked out onto the grimy exterior of the rear of the next building.

Robeson sat in a swivel chair facing them. They sat in old wooden chairs with the varnish long since rubbed off by numerous student bodies. Turner noted the cut of the man's suit, which clung to his body in ways that Turner suspected came from the finest tailoring.

They explained the reason for their visit.

Robeson spoke in a pleasant tenor. "I got a call from Ian. I trust him." He pointed at Turner. "He said you're gay, but that your partner isn't."

"Is that important?" Turner asked.

"That's for you to decide. A gay cop seems suspicious to me on general principles."

Fenwick said, "If you want to give him a morals lecture or your opinion on which profession he should have chosen, why don't you do that and then we can get on with what we came to ask."

Robeson gazed at Fenwick calmly. The silence between them built until the lawyer said, "I guess you're right. What can I tell you?"

"Do you know anything about Donald Mucklewrath being gay?" Turner said.

"It's been a rumor for a while. He's not married and he's in his thirties."

"Always a sure sign," Turner said.

Robeson smiled. "Yeah, that and going to the opera." He cleared his throat. "Anyway, I never paid much attention to the rumors. I assumed it was wishful thinking on the part of a few gay activists who would enjoy the irony of a prominently homophobic person's kid turning out to be gay. Frankly, I'd enjoy it too, but I think the possibility is remote. I certainly have no proof." He shrugged his shoulders, then asked: "I'm curious. How would his being gay be connected to his sister's murder?"

"I honestly don't know," Turner said. "We're looking for any kind of information we can get on the family. If he was being outed, maybe it had a strong effect on those people."

"Our group isn't into outing. That kind of thing is bullshit. People have the right to lead their own lives. We fight to improve the lives of gay people in a lot of ways, but not that shit." He gave them a lecture about the good things his group had done with legislation, lawsuits, and domestic-partner insurance regulations.

They left a few minutes later with no further information. In the car Turner said, "Let's go ask him."

"Him who?" Fenwick said.

"Donald."

"We're going to walk in and ask him if he's gay?"

"Why not?" Turner asked.

In the Mucklewrath suite they found Donald in the company of his stepmother, and they told him they wanted to ask him some questions alone. He and Mrs. Mucklewrath insisted he not be alone. Turner didn't press the issue.

Fenwick asked, "Donald, is it true that you're gay and you killed your sister because she was blackmailing you?"

Donald looked confused and said, "Uh, what?"

Mrs. Mucklewrath shouted, "How dare you? What kind of nonsense is this? How dare you barge in to ask such insulting questions? The police commissioner will hear about this!"

"Superintendent," Fenwick said. "In Chicago we have a police superintendent."

Mrs. Mucklewrath positioned herself a foot away from Fenwick and stabbed her finger at him. "I'll have your badge for this!" she threatened.

"Stars," Fenwick said. "In Chicago we don't call them badges. We call them stars."

She stormed from the room.

Fenwick said, "Well, she isn't always the 'ice maiden,' is she?"

They turned to Donald. Turner asked, "Are you gay?"

Donald looked at him dubiously. "No. I can't imagine where you heard that. I've had lots of women. That's why I'm in trouble, remember?"

"You wouldn't be the first to try to cover up his sexuality by dating women," Turner said.

Donald stood up. He said quietly, "I'm not gay."

A voice spoke behind them. "He certainly isn't."

They turned. The Reverend Mucklewrath stood in the doorway with his wife next to him. An uncomfortable few minutes followed before Turner and Fenwick retreated to the elevator and then the street far below.

The sky remained clear as they walked back to their car, but the wind was up, and with the canyons and eddies the buildings created, they found themselves almost having to bend into the wind.

When they settled into the car Turner said, "I think I believe him. I'm fairly good at knowing if somebody's lying or not. I think he told us the truth."

"You sure?"

"No."

The radio crackled to life. A disembodied voice asked for Turner. He clicked in to respond. "They want you at home," said the voice. "It's something about your kids. A Mrs. Talucci called."

Turner instantly thought of the threats made to his boys. He dropped all thoughts of the murder investigation.

In seconds Fenwick had the siren screaming and the car

roaring through the traffic. At Carpenter Street Turner leaped from the car before it stopped. He raced into the house to find nothing, then tore next door to Mrs. Talucci's. Her eldest daughter, Anna Marie, said, "Family Center Hospital. The school called. We couldn't get hold of you."

She didn't know anything beyond that.

Turner, sitting tightlipped as Fenwick tore down Halsted Street toward the hospital, worried about the possibility that Jeff might have an unexpected problem with his spina bifida. They'd been fortunate the last few years. What was rarely far from the mind of a parent who had a child with the defect was finally happening to him.

Fenwick dropped him at the entrance. Turner, familiar with the hospital, quickly found out where his son was. The nurses on duty recognized him. With their usual brisk efficiency they led him to the operating room. They'd been waiting for him to give approval for an operation.

Jeff's shunt had clogged. Most spina bifida children had the shunt to prevent the buildup of fluid in the brain. Occasionally obstructions worked their way into the opening. Usually there was some warning of a problem, but not always.

He found Mrs. Talucci. She stamped around outside the operating room in a towering rage. She was more furious than he had ever seen her.

Mrs. Talucci said, "It was that goddamn school. They know. How many times have I told them that if they notice anything with Jeff they should call immediately? The teacher this morning thought he had a headache. You don't just 'have a headache' with this kind of child. You watch. You notice." She switched to Italian as she began swearing and berating the school system. She spoke too quickly for Turner to follow all of it. He was pretty sure he missed some of the more obscure obscenities.

Turner had fought with the Chicago education system since before Jeff's first day in school. He wanted his boy to have as normal a life as possible. Mostly the schools weren't set up to deal with anyone unusual or slightly difficult. Most spina bifida children had normal intelligence, but at the least they needed physical therapy and minor assistance. He'd had to argue for the smallest concessions. Administrator after administrator had placed roadblocks in his path. The neighborhood knew and sympathized, but it took Mrs. Talucci on the warpath for things to happen. All she did was ask to accompany Paul to one of his meetings with school personnel. She hadn't said anything until the end. Then she said to them, "I came here today to see. That's all I wanted to do. Look at the people who don't have the kindness or the time for a child. Professional people who are supposed to be working for children." She snorted her derision and left with Paul.

Within a week all the obstacles to Jeff's education had melted away. Once Paul tried to ask Mrs. Talucci what she did, or whom she talked to. All she told him was that she talked to people she knew who cared about kids. She never explained beyond that. If Mrs. Talucci had connections to help his son, Paul didn't care, and he didn't want to know any more.

Mrs. Talucci calmed down very quickly after she spent her initial volley of venom. She sat until the doctor appeared over an hour later and told them Jeff was fine; then she left, and Turner went to see his son. On the way down the corridor he saw George Manfred in a white lab coat, speaking earnestly to a young couple. The doctor finished with the couple and looked up. Turner closed the space between them and quickly filled him in. Manfred accompanied Turner down the corridor.

"What are you doing here?" Turner asked him. "I thought you worked with AIDS patients."

"I've got a couple of kids here and across the street at Children's Hospital. They were born with it."

In the room Turner gently embraced his still-sleeping son. Manfred confirmed what the doctor had said: Jeff would be fine. He promised to come back after his rounds and Turner thanked him, then sat with his boy for over an hour. Jeff had awakened briefly, saw his dad, smiled, and asked for Brian.

At seven Manfred came by. He suggested they grab a bite to eat in the hospital cafeteria. They talked for half an hour about spina bifida and people with AIDS as patients.

97

"Hell of a first date," Turner said as they placed their trays near a stack at the exit to the cafeteria.

"There'll be more and better," Manfred said. Turner watched him walk away. Even with the lab coat he found the view attractive.

He returned to his son's room and sat for another half hour. At eight, Jeff, fully awake and into his favorite TV show, told him, "Dad, you can go home. I'm fine. I get to miss school. So I'm okay." Paul knew the staff would take excellent care of him.

Before he left, he stopped at the hospital's security office and told them of the threats. The man in charge, a retired cop, told him not to worry, that a security guard would be posted by Jeff's room around the clock.

At home he had messages on his answering machine from Fenwick and Ian. Since he had no way to reach Brian at Great America, he called Fenwick. His partner asked about Jeff and Turner filled him in.

Fenwick asked, "You weren't going to check on that outing shit anymore tonight?"

Paul said, "It's not much of a lead, but it'll give me something to do." He knew he shouldn't worry about Jeff, but he probably would. He also knew himself well enough to know he'd probably go through a certain amount of the "Why me?" syndrome, a minor version of the agony he'd gone through at Jeff's birth. Work would help distract him. He called the paper to see if Ian was in, but got an answering machine. He called Ian's apartment and got his roommate. She told him to try John Chester's.

Turner hurried into the humid night. The wind blew at gale force, but still no storms threatened on the horizon. In John Chester's, Turner found Ian singing bawdy songs with a group of pressmen from the Chicago *Tribune*.

Ian saw him and immediately asked, "What's wrong?"

Turner told him about Jeff, finishing: "He's fine, but I'm restless. I figured work will keep me occupied. Better to stay busy than brood." He told Ian what they'd learned about

Donald. "I doubt he's gay," Turner finished, "but I should check every angle."

"Half the time the most virulently homophobic people are the most severely closeted. I met him once or twice. I never pegged him as gay."

"Robeson wasn't much help. I need to talk to the people in the community involved in outing," Turner said.

"I found some information this afternoon. You know some of them as friends. That could be a problem."

"I've got a murder to solve," Turner said. "Maybe several of them. I'm not interested in likes or dislikes at this point."

First Turner called home from the bar to see if Brian was in yet. He got the answering machine, but wasn't worried. On these trips Brian often didn't get in before twelve.

In the car Turner asked, "Where to?"

Ian said, "Gill Garret's place."

"Gill's into outing?" Turner asked.

"Yep," Ian said. "He's one of the leaders."

"I guess I didn't know him as well as I thought."

"Gill doesn't tell a lot of people. There are others who get their name in the paper, but he's the brains behind the outfit."

Gill Garret lounged in a silk bathrobe in front of a TV set, watching reruns of *thirtysomething*.

"Is Donald Mucklewrath gay?" Ian asked him after they'd sat down with drinks, a Diet Coke for Turner.

"How would I know?" Garret took a careful sip from his straight scotch. He leaned back in his recliner, holding his glass in hands folded over his stomach.

Turner said, "He's made a lot of homophobic statements in the press, but we need to check out a rumor we heard."

"He's one of the worst fucking assholes in the country," Garret said. "If he was one of our own, he deserves to be destroyed. One of our own destroying us! I consider that the highest crime you can commit."

Ian put his hand on his friend's arm. "If he's a murderer," he said, "maybe something you know could convict him. We don't want to get anybody in the community in trouble. We want to get the bastard as badly as you do."

Garret wrenched his arm away from Ian. He prowled the room, pausing to stare at a print of a half-naked baseball player hanging on the wall.

Ian asked, "Why all the dramatics? Why not just tell us? It's not that big a secret, is it?"

Finally Gill stopped pacing and faced the two men. He spoke through tight lips. "We've known for about a week. This is our big chance to bust a major homophobe. I know it sounds callous, but I'm not overly concerned about his sister. I'm concerned about the evil he's done to gay people." He sat down. "All right," he said. He sighed. "That little whore, Rusty—the one you had the run in with the other night?—told us. He had a date with some rich bastard a few weeks ago. They went to a party at some mansion in Lake Forest. Rusty said Donald was there with a cute young thing he couldn't keep his hands off. Rusty's one of our main sources in finding out about closeted public officials. The 'old whores' network' we call it. Some of them remain loyal to the code and keep silence. Fortunately, Rusty is one of us."

"He won't last long in the business with a big mouth," Ian said.

"We're very careful, and he's not the only one by any means," Garret said.

"You trust Rusty?" Turner said.

"I have independent confirmation that Donald Mucklewrath was at the party." He took a sip from his drink. "We've been trying to get hold of Donald for a week to set up a meeting. We wanted to talk to him first. We haven't been able to get through. Then, with the murder, our plans got delayed. We're going through with this."

"I guess we should talk to Rusty. Do you know where he is tonight?" Turner asked.

"Working, I suppose. I have no idea where."

Turner and Ian left. The reporter had several suggestions about where they might find a working hustler at ten thirty on a Tuesday night. They tried various bars on Clark Street, then on Halsted, but came up empty.

Finally they stopped at Halsted and Addison and walked into the Eighteenth District police station. Turner identified himself and told them what he needed. He spent nearly half an hour on the phone, finally tracking down someone in Vice Control who specialized in male prostitutes. A Detective Kramer recognized Rusty's name.

"Yeah, Rusty the Drip," she said. "The call him that because supposedly he's given a lot of guys gonorrhea. He's got a larger-than-usual number of unhappy customers. We aren't actually sure why. It could be because of the disease he spreads. Although most of the hustlers we get are heavily into safe sex. Of course, you know how sympathetic we are with a john who comes in complaining about being ripped off by a hustler. We investigate if there's time after the real complaints. You know how often that is."

Turner grunted that he understood. "Do you know where he hangs out?"

"Try the Womb on Clark Street. It's a bar a little south of where you've looked so far. That's his normal hangout."

Inside a crumbling building, luridly decorated and lit barely above fire-code standards, the Womb's clientele slunk furtively from dark corner to dark corner. A year ago they'd removed the Wall, a spotlighted area for viewing the various available young men. Now all lurked together in the same murky depths.

They spotted Rusty conversing with a smiling bald-headed man probably in his sixties or seventies.

Turner walked up behind him and tapped Rusty on the shoulder.

"Fuck off," Rusty said without turning around. The bald man gave Turner an angry stare.

Turner took out his star and showed it to the bald man, who seconds later scuttled out the door. Rusty swung around and Turner said, "Let's go outside."

"Is this a bust?" the kid asked.

"Not yet," Turner said.

Rusty looked at Ian but saw no help from that quarter. He gave his shoulders an elaborate shrug and, swinging his narrow hips suggestively, swung toward the exit.

On the street Turner asked, "What do you know about Donald Mucklewrath?"

"Nothing." The kid leaned against the building, stuck his fingers through several empty belt loops, raised his right foot so the sole of his shoe lay flat against the building. The pose showed his bulging crotch and slender hips to great advantage.

Turner told Rusty what Gill had said.

Rusty sneered and said, "So what?"

With an effort Turner stayed calm and tried reasoning with the kid. Then Ian tried threats about arrest.

The kid laughed at both of them and said, "Let's get the lawyers out here then. I'm sure I'd be happy to talk to one of them. Until then, I got nothing to say."

They gave it up. Turner drove Ian home, then made his way to his own neighborhood. As soon as he walked in the door, he called the hospital. No change in Jeff's condition. The boy was resting comfortably.

It was then he discovered Brian wasn't home yet. It was quarter after twelve. Brian didn't have to be in until one and he rarely broke curfew—Turner was happy he'd had a few problems as he did with his son—but the anxiety of the emergency with Jeff, coupled with the threats, now made him uneasy.

At twelve thirty the phone rang. Brian's voice, barely audible over background noise, said, "Dad, Frank's car broke down. We're at the Deerfield Oasis. We can't fix it. Can you come and get us?"

At one thirty Paul pulled up at the Oasis. Brian and his four buddies sat outside on the curb, looking woebegone and glum. Brian, his pants encrusted with dirt and grease, stood up when he saw his dad's car.

"Sorry, Dad," were his first words.

They checked Frank's 1982 Chevette. After a brief look Paul said, "I can't see the problem. It's too late to try fixing it anyway. Did you all call your parents?"

Everybody nodded except Frank. Turner knew the boy feared his father, and suspected Frank's dad abused him. "Want me to call him, Frank?"

The sixteen-year-old nodded. "He's gonna kill me."

Frank Farnisi grew up with buck teeth and wearing hand-me-down clothing. He'd been a slender little kid and the clothes came from his muscular older brother. His mom's best tailoring efforts couldn't quite disguise the outsized shape of the clothes he wore. The kid had been teased unmercifully. Braces and teenage rebellion, coupled with the best working car among neighborhood teens, had gone a long way toward making up for his earlier unpopularity.

With Frank standing next to him, Turner called. It didn't seem that anybody had noticed Frank wasn't in yet. As Paul explained, Mr. Farnisi came more awake. Paul detected stirrings of anger. Paul tried to smooth the way for the teenager. He wasn't sure how much good he did.

He hung up and Frank said, "Thanks, Mr. Turner."

·On the way home Brian explained what happened. "Frank's car broke down about four miles north of the Oasis. We waited for a tow truck or a cop to stop by. Nobody showed up for forty-five minutes. While we waited, we tried to fix it ourselves. That's how come I'm a mess. None of us is real good at fixing cars. Frank doesn't keep any tools in the car, and we didn't have any light. Finally, a tow truck showed up. We got here and we called you and . . ." He stopped.

Frank finished, "We called you because you're cool, Mr. Turner. We knew you wouldn't get all pissed and go nuts."

"Yeah," Brian said.

Paul yawned. "Could you try and make it a little earlier next time?"

After they dropped the other boys at their homes, Paul told Brian about Jeff. Paul liked the instant concern the older brother expressed for the younger. When they finished discussing Jeff, Paul said, "I should have taken those threats more seriously." He told Brian about the developments. "I want to take as few chances as possible. I'd like you to stay around the house and be as alert and aware as you can."

Brian said, "Do you really think there's any danger?"

"I hope not, but I don't want to risk it. I'd like you to stick close to home. Besides," Paul continued, "the garage needs cleaning and you could spend the next couple days straightening it out."

Brian argued briefly that he was being punished for something he had no control over.

"Okay," Paul said, "we'll work a deal, like usual. I'll help some, if I can." A deal might mean money, but often meant a trade in chores.

Finally at home, on their way upstairs, Turner said, "I'm glad you're okay. I was worried."

Brian mumbled, "Yeah, Dad, I know."

Turner didn't embrace him—his son's teenage ethos prevented that—but he gave Brian's shoulder a paternal squeeze.

The next morning, with less than four hours of sleep, Turner drove to the hospital to check on Jeff. The boy was awake and eating breakfast. He greeted his dad by saying, "Why couldn't this have happened during school? I could have had a good time. Will I have to miss a lot of summer stuff?"

Paul wasn't certain, told him he'd have to ask the doctor. They chatted briefly and then Turner left for work.

At the station everyone asked how Jeff was. They got through roll call with little morning grumbling that day. Too many murders, along with the heat and humidity, kept everyone pretty subdued. Even Carruthers kept quiet for longer than five minutes at a stretch.

Turner reported on his visits the night before. The commander came in and they brought him up to date on all the recent incidents.

"Do you think the Kantakee, Schaumburg, and the Bishop's problems are connected to the murder?"

"Maybe," Turner said. "It could be some new group taking vengeance on some of the most vocal right-wing people around. Tough to make a connection."

He added the information about the nonlethal incidents that Ian had brought to his attention.

At the end the commander said, "Don't close off any assumptions. Investigate the murder and monitor those other problems. It's probably not connected, but you never know, so check it out. Also, I know how this next part screws everything up, but I have to tell you: The political pressure to solve this woman's murder is intense. I'd sure like to be able to report good news soon." He left.

Turner and Fenwick didn't waste time getting angry at the commander. What was the use? He was simply stating a reality they knew all too well.

Turner poured himself some coffee and sat at his desk preparing to start his calls. He wanted to follow up on Ian's information. On top of his desk he found Wilmer's autopsy report. He thumbed through each page.

"Listen to this," he told Fenwick, who'd been hunting for five minutes for a spoon to stir the sugar in his coffee. Fenwick did this every morning. One time Turner tried tying a spoon to the handle of his partner's desk drawer. Fenwick had lost it within fifteen minutes.

"We got part of Wilmer's medical records. He tested positive for HIV antibodies," Turner said.

Fenwick looked up. "Is that what killed him?"

Turner flipped a few pages. "Nope. He didn't drown either. No liquor in his stomach or in his bloodstream. The guy must have been sober. Somebody knocked him over the head. Couldn't have gotten the bump from the fall. If we hadn't been suspicious, we'd probably never have found this out. We need to try to track Wilmer's movements on Saturday. I think he's the key to this whole mess."

Under Wilmer's report, he found a note from the Gang Crimes Unit. He called them, Organized Crime, and Narcotics. He got the same answer from all three. They'd put out feelers and got nothing. Nobody was pissed off at cops this week. Seconds after he hung up, the phone rang. Ian said, "I think we got another one. Down at the Hilton."

S E V E N

Fenwick and Turner ran into massive chaos in the lobby of the Chicago Hilton and Towers. The noted author and talk-show guest Arnold Bennet held court in the grand foyer with a gaggle of media people around him. The camera lights shone on his bald head as he gesticulated and roared.

Arnold Bennet, archconservative and darling of the right wing, published one novel a year, about international conspiracies and foreign intrigue. His books belonged to the more-macho-than-thou-school, with lots of military hardware and international intrigue. His hero, the same now through twenty-six books, bedded a different woman in chapters one, six, and fifteen of each adventure. Every book since number eight had hit the *New York Times* best-seller list. Every book since number seventeen had made it to number one on the list.

Bennet cultivated his reputation as an eccentric. He could show up on a talk show dressed in anything from see-through pajamas to a canary-yellow three-piece suit. He refused to travel on any days except Tuesdays and Thursdays. On the talk shows he loved bantering with hosts and plugging his books. Many criticized him for selling out his profession, but since most of the comments came from authors who were far less successful, they were somewhat suspect.

At the moment, in the lobby of the Hilton, he waved a piece of paper at the cameras; he was, Turner suspected, on the verge of hysteria. They couldn't reach him through the press of reporters, so they listened.

Bennet screeched, "This is all I have left. This is the only thing they left me." He flourished the paper around his head.

A reporter asked, "Why don't you have a copy?"

Bennet stared fixedly at the interlocutor. Turner could barely see either of them through the crush of people. Today Bennet wore an entirely turquoise outfit.

"Everyone knows," Bennet said, superiority dripping from each word, "that I never keep a copy. I never revise. I sit and write until I'm done. I see each instant of action in my mind, and it becomes reality when I put it on paper. Nothing gets between me and my reader. I've never made copies before. I will not in the future."

Turner stopped a hotel employee and asked if he could tell him where to find house security. She pointed to a tall woman at the edge of the mob, behind Bennet. Turner and Fenwick eased around the crowd. Turner showed his star and introduced himself. She jerked her head backward and said, "Follow me."

Away from the press of the crowd she said, "That has to be the biggest jackass this side of anywhere."

"What happened?" Turner asked.

The security director, Mabel Henshaw, told them. "He called us about an hour ago. I think he called the media first. They got here awful goddamn quick. He claims three guys broke into his room. Two of them held him down while the other burned his manuscript. I think it's all just a publicity stunt. Who ever heard of an author keeping one copy of their book?"

Fenwick said, "I've read about this guy. Supposedly it's true. He only keeps one copy. He takes it with him on his tours. Sort of like a security blanket."

"At any rate," Henshaw said, "I can't see it being important enough for you guys to be here."

Turner explained briefly about trying to find connections between odd problems far-right-wing people had been having lately. "Did these guys talk to him?" he asked.

Henshaw said, "I haven't had two minutes alone with him to ask. He started going nuts when the first camera showed up, and he hasn't stopped. You guys can question him if you want."

With Henshaw's assistance they got Bennet away from the cameras. They returned to his hotel room to talk to him.

"How did they get in here?" Turner asked.

"I called room service." Bennet paced up and down the room throughout the conversation, frequently punctuating his statements with wild gestures. "They must have intercepted the call, or the guy with the cart. They came in, grabbed me, and threw me down on the bed."

"How many were there?" Fenwick asked.

"Three. All wore dark sport coats. One was very tall and exceptionally thin. The others were of medium height. They found my manuscript, held it in front of my face, and then burned it. One of them disconnected the smoke alarm before they started. They used the cover of the serving tray to put the ashes in."

"Did they say anything?" Turner asked.

"Yeah. 'Sorry now, aren't you?' What the hell is that supposed to mean?"

"How did they get away?"

"They knocked me out with cholorform. I used it in three or four of my books, and I know the smell. I was out just a few minutes."

"Who would do this kind of thing to you?" Fenwick asked.

"How should I know?"

"Does anyone have reason to dislike you? Have you gotten any threats lately?" Turner asked.

"I always get nasty letters from bleeding-heart liberals. Last year I suggested we create a funeral pyre of all the legislators who opposed the flag-burning amendment to the Constitution. A couple of people have filed suits over the years claiming I slandered them in my books. Just because they see their pet liberal causes or politicians made fun of, they get all huffy. Bleeding-heart wimps can't take it."

"Any specific causes or groups lately?" Turner asked.

He thought a minute. "Nope, nobody lately."

"Was that really your only copy of the next book?" Turner said.

"Yes. I keep only one copy."

"What will you do?" Fenwick asked.

"Find the bastards and torture them as they scream for mercy."

Fenwick said, "I meant about the book."

"I'll have to write it again. The whole goddamn thing."

In the hallway waiting for the elevator Turner said, "Same three guys?"

"Got to be," Fenwick said. He shook his head, "I can't believe that the liberals organized a terrorist group."

"Maybe the meek got tired of waiting," Turner replied. When the elevator reached the first floor he said, "Let's talk to room service."

Down in the kitchen area they found that everything about the order for Bennet had been very normal. He'd called down. They'd made the breakfast and Feliz took the order up to the room. He'd never come back and never delivered the food. The head of the kitchen whispered to them. "Feliz Milta is an illegal. I don't want trouble. We hire some of them to give them a break. Not because it's cheaper. We pay everybody the going wage. He has no green card. He probably saw trouble and ran."

They obtained Feliz's address from payroll and drove to Eighteenth and Ashland.

Feliz answered the door of his fourth-floor walk-up apartment. He saw their stars and shoved the door in their faces. Fenwick caught it and threw it back at him. Feliz staggered and then tried to run. Turner caught him halfway down a hallway. Feliz struggled briefly but Turner, younger and stronger, subdued him in less than a minute.

They cuffed him and sat him down on a kitchen chair. Feliz spoke accented English; he was about five foot five, with cropped black hair. Turner guessed him to be in his late forties.

Feliz refused to look at them when they asked questions. Finally Turner said, "Feliz, we don't want to send you back to Mexico. We just want to find out why you didn't bring up that tray this morning."

"Why should I believe you?" Feliz asked.

Turner said, "Look at me."

The man raised his brown eyes to look at Turner.

"I give you my word. You tell us what we want to know, and we leave. We forget we ever knew you."

Feliz gazed at Turner for over a minute, weighing his chances. Finally he said, "If I don't talk?"

"We bust your ass," Fenwick said.

Feliz shrugged. "I get a lousy deal, or I got to trust you? Some choice."

Turner did something genuinely shocking. He caught Feliz's eyes and said, "Please."

Feliz Milta's jaw dropped in disbelief.

Turner asked, "Why didn't you bring up the tray?"

"Three guys stopped me in the hallway outside the room. They offered me money to let them take care of it. When I heard what happened later, I ran."

"What did they look like?" Turner asked.

Feliz shut his eyes and thought. "They looked like North Americans. White."

"Did you notice eye color, height, weight?" Turner asked.

He gave the same general description as Bennet had, and little more. "They offered me a lot of money, and I didn't bother to notice anything else."

"How much did they offer?" Fenwick said.

Feliz gazed about nervously.

"We aren't going to steal it from you," Turner said.

Feliz said, "A lot of money." He looked at Turner's face. "Five hundred dollars."

Fenwick said, "Not a bad day's pay."

"What else did they say?" Turner asked.

"Nothing. They told me there would be no trouble and I

1 1 0

could keep the money no matter what. With that much I can help my family here and in Mexico."

"Did you see them later?" Turner asked.

"No. I took the money and left. I wanted to hide it in case they changed their minds and tried to accuse me of stealing it."

Turner unlocked the handcuffs.

Feliz eyed them suspiciously. "You are really going to let me go?"

"You haven't done anything illegal that we need to handle. Be careful with the money," Turner said. They left.

In the car Fenwick said, "I still can't believe you said please. Now we ask politely?"

"I thought it might work with this guy," Turner said, "and it did."

"We should have busted him, or brought him in to look at mug shots," Fenwick said.

"Probably, and the money could have some bearing on the case, but my guess is it was all in small unmarked bills. If we need it, we can come back and get it. Mug shots are useless. These guys are new on the block."

"What if Feliz skips?"

Turner eyed his partner. "We could arrest him. For now I'm willing to take a chance. I doubt we'd find the money. He's got it hidden. Besides, we promised the guy. I'd rather keep my word."

Fenwick grunted agreement. "We going to try to track Wilmer's movements."

Turner nodded. "He lived on Lake Street, a few blocks west of Racine."

"How do you know that?"

"I've been there. A couple of whores rolled him one night. He looked worse than usual. It was after his weekly dousing with perfume. I saw him on the street and took him home. He lives in one of the abandoned buildings down there."

Fenwick said, "We should have listened to him. I should have listened to him. He must have known something."

"Or he got rolled by some bored kids who dumped him into the river for the hell of it. Let's go."

Two buildings, separated by a narrow gangway, sat amid the debris of a torn-down block on the near West Side. At eleven in the morning they didn't have the sinister emptiness of midnight fears. El tracks stretched overhead. They banged on the door of the building farther east.

"It's abandoned," Turner said.

Fenwick kicked at the door. It fell in on the second blast. Dust motes scattered upward as they climbed the stairs in front of them. Scraps of wood paneling, remnants of what once lined the walls halfway to the top, remained in scattered strips. They heard no rustling of human occupation; no radios or TVs, no other debris of the electronic age, intruded on their trudge up the stairs. Oppressive humidity and closeness surrounded them.

"Why'd he have to live on the top floor?" Fenwick said as they paused on the landing outside his door. "Awful goddamn dark in here," he added. "I should go back for the flashlight."

Turner shrugged. He pushed at the door and it opened. A window, smeared with filth to the point of opacity, let in only enough light to prevent a trek down for the flashlight. The paint on the walls of the apartment matched the top half of the ones in the hall—barren, encrusted with dirt and soot, perhaps painted light yellow in a better time.

The one room had no appliances and no bathroom. It stank of piss and shit, although neither were in blatant evidence. The mattress from a twin bed lay in one corner. A tattered blanket sat in a heap in the middle of the bed.

Next to it they found two boxes. From the first one, Turner pulled out a plastic trophy that said Wilmer had been the checkers champion of Crawfordsville, Indiana, when he was in sixth grade. Fenwick pulled out a bag that contained marbles: three steelies and two extra-large cat-eyes, along with fourteen assorted smaller ones. They sifted through the other materials but turned up nothing of value to the investigation.

In the second box Turner found a collection of broken and

ruined toy cars. "Poor guy," Turner said. He explained to Fenwick about Wilmer's presents for Jeff.

They removed the cars, under which they found a variety of papers. The two men sat on the edge of the mattress. Fenwick moved the tattered blanket out of the way with the tips of two fingers. They each took a stack of papers and examined them carefully.

"I think this is a high-school diploma from someplace in Indiana," Fenwick said. "Maybe Crawfordsville, but I can't really make it out." He turned to the next one. "These are medical notices."

Turner glanced at them. He said, "These are all from Mother Mary Hospital. We can start there. Most of this is just paperwork. We can take it with us." At the bottom of the papers they found a faded black-and-white photo. A young child looked out at them in a sailor suit in front of what was probably a zoo cage. Fenwick said, "I wonder if that's him or his kid."

Turner peered at the picture. "From the style of the clothes, I'd say it's him."

They drove to Mother Mary Hospital, noted throughout the West Side of the city for its charitable work. The vast complex stood near the corner of Ashland and North Avenues. Half of it looked ready to collapse into the nearby slums. The other half looked as if it would be the envy of most of the medical centers in the country.

The nun in charge, Sister Constance, greeted them warmly. Turner explained to her about the autopsy report on Wilmer and showed her the papers they found in the apartment. He concluded, "We'd like to know who his doctor was, especially the names of any friends or even personal contacts among the hospital staff."

She examined the papers for several minutes. "These do say he tested positive for HIV antibodies." She frowned and shuffled through them again. "There's no record here that he ever accepted AZT or any other treatment. Also that he never had any opportunistic infections." She turned to her computer and pressed keys rapidly for a minute then looked at them. "What you have here is a fairly complete record."

Turner asked, "Is it strange, that he didn't accept treatment?"

"It's a little odd, but some of our older patients refuse treatment. Some of them want to die, or think they do. Often they turn to us when it's too late."

"Did he have any family?" Turner asked.

Sister Constance ran her fingers rapidly over the keyboard. "Nothing listed here."

"Was he seeing any doctor in particular?" Turner asked.

She worked the computer a few seconds, then said, "Dr. Schemeil or Dr. Manfred."

"Is that George Manfred?" Turner asked.

"Yes, do you know him?" the nun asked.

"We've met."

"He's one of our best doctors. Spends all his time with the people with AIDS. Does a wonderful job with them and their families. Works incredible hours."

"Anyone else Wilmer talked to on a regular basis?" Turner asked.

"You can try down in the emergency room. They get to know some of the regulars, and according to the records your Wilmer was in and out. Drunks fall down and hurt themselves often."

After finding out that Dr. Schemeil was on vacation and Dr. Manfred wouldn't be in, they interviewed the emergency-room staff. A few vaguely remembered Wilmer, but none knew him well. As Turner and Fenwick got ready to leave, an older nurse, in her sixties and moving slowly as if her feet hurt and there were a million miles to go before the end of her shift, introduced herself as May Worth and said she knew Wilmer. She beckoned for them to follow to a small staff lounge area. She got her coffee and plunked onto a gray couch, then said, "I knew him. Tough old coot. Never wanted anybody to touch him. Didn't like me because I made him clean up whenever he came in. I washed that old man's body more time than I care to admit." She sipped her coffee.

Turner felt that if he ever needed to have a nurse, he wanted to have one exactly like May Worth.

She continued, "I used to talk to him. Did you know he graduated from Harvard?"

Turner said, "A lot of bums make claims."

"You're telling me. And you're saying I can't tell the difference? I've been doing this forty years, since before either of you was born. I've seen poor people, rich people, frightened people, dying people, brave people. These old bones have seen a lot of death and dying, and miracles too. I've seen people at their best and worst and I'm here to tell you when Wilmer talked to me, I learned the truth. He tried lies. They all do. I have my ways. I listen; most people don't. You ever stop to listen to him?"

"Not often enough," Turner said.

"Too bad. You might have learned something."

Turner cleared his throat. "Did he tell you anything about friends or relatives?"

"I know he was married once. Don't know where or for how long. Came to Chicago in the early fifties, couldn't get a job. Used to mumble that Joe McCarthy ruined him. Never had any visitors when he stayed overnight. You might talk to Dr. Manfred. He might have known him better. He's a good doctor. Has a good relationship with the patients. They trust him."

"Did Wilmer make friends here at the hospital?" Turner asked.

"A few. He liked to talk. He was most friendly with the most seriously ill PWAs. Many of the ones he used to talk to are dead. Nobody who's here now."

In the hall they used the phone at the nurse's station to call Manfred's answering service.

"Why do you have his number?" Fenwick said.

"He's the guy I met," Turner said.

"Oh," Fenwick said, then added, "We'll have to check the other shifts here."

Turner agreed. They'd have to come back.

They waited five minutes for Manfred to return his page. While waiting, Fenwick ogled the female hospital personnel.

Manfred greeted Turner effusively when he found out who it was. When he found out what it was, he suggested they meet at Family Care Hospital when Turner made his afternoon visit. "I've got a couple of kids I need to stop by and see," Manfred told him.

Back at Area Ten they tackled the paperwork.

At five Ian called.

"I don't want to hear this, do I?" Turner asked.

"I'm going with the biggest scoop of my career. No one else has put all these incidents together. Only a gay paper would monitor such things. We watch the conservatives here. Have to, so we know what the opposition is up to. The reverend called another news conference to denounce just about everybody, especially gay people. If it is a gay conspiracy to destroy some right-wing assholes, I have mixed feelings about it. A story like that could be really bad press for the gay community. On the other hand it would make a terrific story. At any rate, I intend to find out the truth, no matter who's responsible."

"Be careful," Turner warned. He understood Ian being torn between loyalty to the community and his journalistic integrity. "The murder is difficult enough to solve without these right wing people trying to blame the gay community for a crime, which I doubt gays committed. These other things you've told me about haven't helped. Murderers do not do pranks."

"You got a better explanation?"

"Several. All involving coincidences, which doesn't make a lot of sense either." He sighed. "I just want to solve the cases."

"You can have honor and glory forever."

"I'd rather just do my job," Turner said.

At six, still mired in paperwork, Turner and Fenwick decided to call it quits. They drove separate cars up to the hospital. Fenwick would drive home right from the interview with Manfred.

In Jeff's room, Brian perched on the empty second bed, chatting cheerfully on the phone. Several books lay on the bedcovers near Jeff's right side. Turner saw that one of them was *Freddy and the Popinjay* by Walter R. Brooks. A game of

Monopoly rested on the tray that swung out to be used for eating. Houses and hotels covered numerous properties. Mrs. Talucci sat in a chair reading Descartes' *Philosophical Essays.* George Manfred stood by Jeff's left side, talking animatedly with the boy.

Jeff saw his dad first. "Hey, Dad, I finally beat Brian at Monopoly."

Brian put his hand over the phone receiver and said, "He got lucky."

Turner ruffled his younger son's hair and congratulated him on his victory. He heard Brian tell whoever was on the other end of the line that he had to go. Mrs. Talucci smiled at Turner. Turner introduced Manfred and Fenwick.

Turner checked on his son's progress with a nurse who entered in answer to his pressing the button. Jeff would be able to leave the hospital soon.

After talking briefly with his sons and Mrs. Talucci, Turner, Fenwick, and Manfred moved into the hallway.

They asked him about Wilmer.

"I heard he died," Manfred said. "I've been trying to find out from what. I couldn't learn anything. I didn't think it was AIDS. I heard he got drunk and fell off a bridge. Is that right?"

"No," Turner said. He told him what they knew.

"Who'd want to murder an old drunk?"

"We aren't sure," Turner said. "We're trying to trace him movements that last Saturday, but we don't know who his buddies were."

"I can't help you much. I know his favorite place to flop was the Mission of Eternal Peace."

"Mucklewrath's mission?" Fenwick said.

"Pardon me?" Manfred said.

Fenwick explained briefly.

Manfred knew little about Wilmer's private life. "If you've talked to May Worth, you know as much as almost anybody in the hospital. That woman is worth more than an entire school of brain surgeons."

Fenwick left to go home. Manfred said he had a few more

117

kids to see, and maybe they'd have time to talk briefly when he got back.

Turner reentered his son's room. Brian and Jeff sat on the bed with the Monopoly board set up for a new game. They played intently, each determined to win.

Mrs. Talucci left her paperback on the seat of the chair. She motioned Turner back into the hall.

She whispered, "You know that Dr. Manfred?"

Turner nodded. "We've met a couple times."

"I like him. He's not an Italian boy, but that's all right. He was good with Jeffy. But have you talked to Ben Vargas yet?"

"We always talk, Mrs. Talucci."

"You haven't asked him for a date yet?"

"No, Mrs. Talucci."

"Nice Italian boys are the kind to settle down with. This Manfred though, that doesn't sound Italian. Although he is a doctor, I like that."

"We haven't really even gone out on a date." Why was he explaining this to her, he thought. Then again, why not. She cared.

Turner decided to stop by the Mission of Eternal Peace on his way home. An enormous renovated factory building housed the mission, on west Madison Street two blocks east of Chicago Stadium, where the Bulls played their home games. Inside Turner found secretaries at computer terminals, well-polished floors, and gleaming woodwork. The people he saw moved with purpose and efficiency. A well-scrubbed young man in a form-fitting, short-sleeved white shirt and black pants greeted him from behind a modern desk. Turner showed his star and asked to talk to whoever was in charge at the moment. Several days ago he'd talked to a Mrs. Epstein. The young man brought Turner to her again.

She smiled in greeting. He told her he wanted to find out information about Wilmer.

"I don't know our clients by name. You might find a few of the staff who know him. May I take you to them?"

He agreed. As they left her office, another gleaming modern room, she asked if he wanted a tour. For half an hour Turner let her lead him around the entire complex. The old factory must have taken over half a city block, and not an inch of it hadn't been cleaned and polished to a shine. Much of it had been rehabbed and some was completely new. She showed him chapels, work rooms, dormitories for men and women, dining rooms, a library, custodian's closets, and storage rooms. Everything seemed neat and organized in the extreme. Turner began to appreciate the kind of scale the reverend worked on. It would take millions in donations to subsidize such an operation, even if every one of the workers was a volunteer. All of these appeared to be young and energetic.

In their slouched stupors the homeless, gathered at various parts of the building, seemed mostly overwhelmed at their surroundings.

"Who would have had the most contact with Wilmer?" Turner asked.

She led him to a large admitting room. "Each person who comes in has to sign in here. They are assigned their task for their stay. We don't give anything away free. They have no money, but they can give us their strong arms and bodies to clean, sweep, whatever is needed."

Another young man, who could have been the twin to the receptionist, stood up and shook Turner's hand. Mrs. Epstein said to him, "Travis, help the detective in any way you can. If you can't, please see if any of the others have any information he needs."

The youth nodded, smiled at Turner. Travis sat on the edge of the desk. Turner wondered if the boy's face ever began to crack from what seemed to be a permanent smile. Immediately upon thinking this, he berated himself. The kid probably worked hard in an environment that had to be foreign to him. He must have seen and heard enough to depress him for the rest of his life. Turner had grudging admiration for faith that could stand up to the beating it must take every day, even in this gleaming, well-financed facility.

"How long have you worked here, Travis?" Turner asked.

"About a year. I go to the U. of I. during the day. I make a little money doing this. They have a tuition program here for the employees, for us kids in the faith. Have you been saved, Mr. Turner?"

Turner said, "I need to ask about one of the homeless who used to use the shelter, Wilmer Pinsakowski. He's been murdered. You know him?"

The boy looked genuinely shocked. "What happened?" he asked.

"Somebody bashed him on the head and threw him into the river," Turner said.

"Old Wilmer? What on earth for? He was the most harmless guy. He never got in any fights or anything. He never complained about the work we gave him to do." Travis shook his head. "He was one of the great characters around here. Everybody knew him. He spent one or two nights a week. I don't think he needed the place to stay, but he came for the meals. A lot of the people here have places to sleep, but they don't have enough to get something to eat, and it's easier to stay here than trudge to some miserable flop. Plus we have air conditioning."

"How was he a great character?"

"He told the best stories. A lot of times our clients exaggerate, or even fabricate entire lives and it's all lies, but Wilmer, he told stories. People would gather around to listen to him, and somehow he got them to tell fewer lies about their lives. Lots of them trusted Wilmer."

"Anybody in particular?"

"No," Travis said, "just most everybody."

"What time did he come in Friday?"

"Around eleven. A little late for him, but not all that unusual. Some of the shelters close early. We never do."

"Had he been around much lately?"

"Not the past few days, but I'm not always on duty."

"When was the last time you saw him?"

"Friday night, I think. It was a fairly slow night. Many of them sleep outside in the summer. We have fewer people, so it's easier to notice."

"How did he seem that night?"

"How do you mean?"

"Did he act normal?"

The boy thought a minute. "No, not really. I mean, he didn't tell stories. When he came in, he always teased me, and he didn't that night."

"What would he tease you about?"

Travis blushed red. He stared at his feet. "He tried to talk dirty to me. They teach us to ignore a lot of the stuff the clients say. A lot of them are disturbed in the head, and they say all kinds of crazy things." He looked up at Turner. "I think," he whispered, "Wilmer may have been a homosexual. He made comments about my pants and other stuff. I never said anything. We're not supposed to let that type in, but Wilmer was a good guy. I've never met a real homosexual."

Turner resisted the impulse to say "Now you have."

Travis continued, "That night he didn't tease me. He just got his admittance pass and his work assignment."

"Did he have any friends?"

"None of them really had friends."

"Anybody he talked to more than the others?"

Travis scratched his nearly brush-cut hair. "Well, he used to talk with Ajax. They had work detail together that night. They had to scrub the front hall. Ajax hates to work so we try to pair him up with somebody we can reasonably trust. Less supervision on our part."

"Ajax is his real name?"

"We never question them. Many are ashamed of what they've become. We accept what they say. We really don't need more than that."

"Ajax here?"

"I'm not sure. Sometimes he gets here early. He just got thrown out of his regular place. They tend to feel real lost when they lose a familiar spot, even if it's just an old refrigerator carton behind an old building." Travis checked the sign in list. "Yep. He's here. He's assigned to trash detail."

No one had seen Ajax for half an hour. They began a search. They found him curled up and snoring in one of the pews in the chapel. The man's white-streaked gray hair was down to his shoulders; he wore a stained and torn army jacket that might have been issued to him in World War II.

Travis introduced them and left. Turner showed Ajax his star, but the half-awake man barely seemed to notice.

Instead he said, "I don't talk to cops." Ajax's rusty tenor had a tendency to crack like a teenage boy's.

Turner sat in the pew with Ajax, keeping only a foot or so between them. "Why not?" Turner asked.

"Don't trust them. They never help out. Always want to harass you and make fun." He spent some minutes letting Turner know his view of cops in particular and then of the world in general. He eyed Turner suspiciously as he finished, "How come you don't yell at me and tell me you're going to run me in if I don't talk?"

"Because I won't do that."

Ajax cackled loudly. The sound echoed off the stark white walls. "Sorry, young man," he said when he got himself under control. "I don't believe you."

"I'm here about Wilmer," Turner said quietly.

Ajax got teary-eyed. "I heard he died. He was the only one here who ever cared for anybody else. Always collecting his damn toy cars. If any of us ever found any, we always had to give them to him. He had his damn collection. Said he needed it for a little crippled kid he knew. He didn't know any crippled kid."

Turner said, "He never met my son, but he knew about him."

"You got a crippled kid?"

Turner said, "My son Jeff has a birth defect."

Ajax rubbed the stubble on his chin with the back of his right hand. The lines of old scars covered the front of the palm. Turner noted the encrusted dirt blackening the edges of all Ajax's fingernails. The old man leaned close. Turner didn't flinch from the odor and the blast of noxious breath as Ajax said, "You're Turner?"

"Travis introduced us when we found you," Turner reminded him.

"I was asleep. You guys startled me. I didn't know you were that Turner. Wilmer always talked about you and your kid. He wanted a perfect collection of cars to give to the boy. He liked you. Talked about you."

Turner watched the old man carefully.

"How come you got a crippled little boy?" Ajax asked.

The one question Paul had asked himself ten thousand times after his son's birth. The one he'd never gotten an answer for. The question he'd taught himself not to ask. Now brought to the fore by this old man, the memory stung as if it were the night Jeff was born.

Turner placed his elbows on his knees, his body facing forward, but his head turned sideways so he could look at the man next to him. "I don't know," Turner said slowly. "My wife died giving birth to him."

Ajax placed his hand on Turner's shoulder. The cop didn't flinch. "I heard a lot of claims," the old man said. "I know which are true. I believe yours." He coughed and peered around the chapel. The brown pews, a simple metal lectern, and the parquet floor barely relieved the starkness of the four white surrounding walls.

"I better tell you about Wilmer," Ajax said.

Turner nodded.

"He had AIDS. He couldn't tell anybody here. They wouldn't let him in. Wilmer hadn't been eating much lately. He'd lost a lot of weight."

Turner gave an encouraging grunt.

"Didn't bother me any. I'm not prejudiced about sick people, or if they like guys."

Turner almost smiled at the wreck of humanity next to him confessing his liberality.

"Something bothered him Friday night. Bothered him bad."

123

Turner waited while the old man coughed and brushed away some spittle from the side of his mouth.

"He wanted to talk to you. I'm surprised he didn't. Said he was going to."

"He tried to," Turner said. He found himself describing the scene outside the police station where Wilmer had gotten angry and left before telling what he knew.

"Typical cops," Ajax said. "Although you don't seem to be a bad sort. Anyway, he had to talk to you. He claimed he knew something about that murdered girl. He wouldn't tell me what. I know he had a big-deal meeting with someone Saturday. Don't know with who. Wilmer said he'd give you one more try after the meeting."

"Did he say with whom or where?"

Ajax thought long and hard. "Nope, sorry. If he mentioned it, I can't remember."

"Could it have been an HIV-positive support group or anything like that?" Turner asked.

"Nope," Ajax said. "He didn't like groups. Always said he liked people, but put 'em in a group and they start making rules for each other. Nope. No group."

After a few more minutes of questioning Turner said, "If you think of anything, will you call me?"

"I talked an awful lot for free tonight," Ajax said.

Turner looked at the old man. "I appreciate what you've told me. I'll do what I can to pay you back for talking to me, but I can't promise you anything."

Ajax laughed. "At least you're honest, young fella. Most everybody else would have promised me a bottle at least. I like you, I think."

A light rain fell while Turner drove from the Mission home. He wished it would rain hard enough to cool the weather off.

As Turner pulled onto Taylor Street from Racine, he saw three blue-and-white police cars double-parked near the lemonade stand. These added to the normal confusion of the crowded street. He looked to see what the problem was. He saw people sitting on the stoops, gathered at the corners, a few lounging on top of mailboxes, the normal activity of a miserably hot summer night. He didn't see any of the cops. He pulled into his street. His house blazed with light. A beat cop gestured at him angrily. Turner didn't recognize the guy, who now started to yell at him to get his fucking car out of the way. Fire trucks pulled up behind him silently as Turner leaped from his car. He shoved his star at the screamer and began to race toward his house. Halfway down the street the voice of Mrs. Talucci, mixed with a few he began to recognize from the local district, stopped him. He hurried toward a knot of police huddled in the shadows in front of Mrs. Talucci's house.

E I G H T

Mrs. Talucci brushed aside several large, beefy sergeants and spoke quietly. "I called the police about ten minutes ago. I saw three men lurking in the alley behind your house. They tried to get inside by the back door. I don't think Brian heard them. I called your house. Brian was upstairs. I told him to lock himself in the bathroom. Two minutes before the police showed up, the men disappeared around the other side of the house."

"We don't know if they got in or not," a lieutenant said. "We've got every car in the district within a three-block radius of here. I told them to pick up anybody who looks the least bit out of place."

Turner looked at the crowd gathered at the end of the street. He thought that if these guys were smart, if they hadn't gotten into the house, they'd mingle with the crowd and not try to get away. He turned his gaze back to his home. "I'm going in," he said.

A lieutenant, a captain, and two sergeants argued, quoted hostage procedures to him. If these were killers, and they'd gotten in, people could get hurt, and they didn't know where Brian was. Turner knew he was going in. He waited for a distraction to pull the others' attention away from the scene, and got it a few minutes later when a camera crew from one of the local TV stations pulled up. They immediately tried to move as close to the scene as possible. A minor shoving match developed when the zeal of both reporters and cops reached an aggressive stage. As the assembled brass's attention wavered, Turner moved.

Carefully and quietly, he approached his home. He'd lived here most of his thirty-five years. He'd grown up knowing the cracks and crevices of every inch of this space. On the dark side of the porch he found the old waterspout he used to climb down as a twelve-year-old, sneaking out on warm nights just like this one to watch the adults and older kids perform the magic rites of summer up and down Taylor Street.

He'd reinforced the gutters and spouts two years ago. As silently as he had done twenty-three years ago, he scrambled up the side. Hearing muffled curses behind him, he felt more than saw other figures now silently move toward the house. He gouged his hand as he swung himself onto the top of the porch. Blood oozed from the wound.

Facing the sidewalk the rooms proceeded: Brian's bedroom, his bathroom, and Turner's own bedroom.

He landed near Brian's bedroom window and called his son's name softly. No answer. He listened intently. Sounds from the street and the crowd, nothing from inside. He knew he wouldn't be able to break into any of the windows or screens. They could only be opened by a special catch inside, which he had installed himself, so he knew they'd hold.

Inch by inch he moved his head so that he could see into his son's room. Through the screen he observed the room's contents. Two footballs and three baseball bats strewn across the bed, at least six pairs of athletic shoes scattered around the floor, a pile of odoriferous gym clothes in a corner. All definitely undisturbed by human presence at the moment.

The roof of the porch still felt warm to his touch from the heat of the day. He crawled along the tar paper to the next window. This would be the bathroom closest to Brian's room,

127

the nearest place with a lock on the door, if he'd been up here when the call came.

Paul wiped the still-oozing blood from his hand on his shirt—he'd abandoned his suit coat in the car—crouched under the windowsill, and again called his son's name softly. He held his breath, then called again. A moment later he heard a soft "Dad?"

Paul whispered, "It's me, Brian. Open the window, as carefully and quietly as you can."

A minute later he saw Brian's face appear. His son's broad shoulders made it a tight squeeze, but seconds later he crouched next to his dad. Paul put a hand on his son's shoulder. "You okay?"

"Yeah, I think so. What's going on, Dad? Mrs. Talucci talked half in Italian. I couldn't understand all of it, just the part about hiding."

Brian sounded a little shaken, but seemed generally okay.

"Somebody might be trying to get into the house."

"Holy shit! Good thing Jeff's not here. We'd have to go in and rescue him."

Paul grinned at the youthful daring of his older son. The cops below called up to them. With silence now less vital, they talked in normal tones. Brian climbed down as if he knew exactly where to go. Turner didn't want to know how the teenager moved across the roof so easily and quickly.

Minutes later the cops rushed the house. They found it empty. After fifteen minutes of fruitless search, which included Paul and Brian thoroughly examining the house, a sergeant on the street remarked, "It was probably a false alarm."

Unfortunately for him, Mrs. Talucci heard the comment. Fortunately, Turner was close by and halted her attack. Few things stopped Mrs. Talucci, definitely not a police sergeant only twice her size.

After Turner had calmed Mrs. Talucci down, the two of them stood in a cluster of police brass and discussed the possibilities. A beat cop approached them and said, "We got at least three other calls, all within minutes of each other, reporting the same thing. That's one of the reasons help came so quick, plus someone said it was a cop's house."

Mrs. Talucci beamed. She'd been around long enough to know what makes cops move.

The beat cop also said, "We found somebody down at the end of the alley. He says he saw three guys run out of here about half an hour ago."

"He get a description?" Turner asked.

"White males, one tall, two shorter. Ran down Polk Street. We're canvassing the neighbors down that way to see if anybody saw anything."

The commander drove up. Apprised of the situation, he arranged for a cop outside the house until further notice.

By one o'clock the neighborhood had calmed down. Paul spent a half hour talking to Brian. The kid seemed more excited than scared. Before they went to bed, Paul reminded him that he needed to start on his regular summer chores tomorrow, now that the garage was clean. This night he got only minor teenage complaints about the unfairness of housework.

Tired though he was from lack of sleep Tuesday, Paul Turner slept little that night. He tried listening to the soothing prattle of an all-news station. He learned the temperature wouldn't drop below eighty overnight and would rise to the high nineties tomorrow. He kept his gun loaded in the top drawer of the nightstand for the first time in his fifteen years as a cop. He lay awake imagining the horror of losing one of his sons. Around three he almost called the hospital to check on Jeff, but realized he was being paranoid. He'd worked with them before, and he trusted the security force at the hospital.

He knew whoever was after them had to be an amateur. A criminal who wanted a case to be dropped had to warn off an entire department or had to have enough clout to get an investigation called off from the top, and in a murder case it would be extremely difficult, even for someone incredibly well connected. So whoever did it couldn't be well connected and

129

didn't know police procedure. He kept in mind Ian's gay-conspiracy angle, but he knew there were far more likely possibilities.

"You look like hell," Fenwick said to him the next morning.

Turner explained the attempted attack on his house last night.

Fenwick said, "Double and triple fuck. Who are these people?"

At roll call they discussed the murder, the pranks against right wing people, and the attack. Many of the detectives offered opinions and advice. None had a solution.

"Anything unusual in the Mucklewrath camp?" Turner asked.

Wilson said, "I got the report as I came in from the stakeout. Absolutely nothing. I went to last night's rally. Do you guys know he now keeps an urn with his daughter's ashes in front of the speakers' platform? He refers to it in his speech. He works the crowd up, which I guess is pretty normal, then he talks about his daughter. Ninety thousand people and not a dry eye in the bunch."

"He uses his daughter?" Fenwick asked.

"Absolutely. It's pretty sick, but I bet the coffers are overflowing."

"We should get on the angle that someone is taking revenge on him," Turner said. "It's got to be someone he's hurt or who knows him. Who's doing background on him?"

Rodriguez raised his hand. "I've got nothing so far."

"Try some more digging. Anything in his background anywhere might help."

"It's tough," Rodriguez said, "they've got his life compartmentalized. If they don't want you to know it, it's not around. He may have come across as open to you, but his organization is tighter than any group I've ever dealt with."

"Keep trying," Turner said. "Also let's expand the research to other prominent preachers. Somebody's got to have a grudge against him. Get somebody to help you with it."

The lieutenant added, "This is top priority. Somebody's after Paul's kids. That's bullshit."

Generally detectives didn't have time to do the investigations people expected from watching TV shows. The workload for real cops was too great, and often in-depth checking wasn't necessary. Statistically the vast majority of non-gang-related killings were done by someone close to the victim, friend or relative, fairly easy to identify. Because of Mucklewrath's prominence and the play the media gave his daughter's murder, they would get more attention than most. Maybe this wasn't fair but it was certainly reality.

"Are the killings and these pranks really related?" Wilson asked.

They all looked at Turner. "I don't know. We've got two senseless murders. The preacher's daughter and Wilmer."

"You can't discount those prank incidents," Rodriguez said. "They may not be murder, but you've got the similar messages."

Turner shook his head. "Could be copycats. It's starting to be too many coincidences. I can't prove it, but my instincts say they aren't related."

The lieutenant said, "You're going to have to explore that angle. It's weird, but who knows?"

Carruthers said, "You're not really connecting the death of the old shit Wilmer with these, are you? He was old, ignorant, and somebody told me he had AIDS. Who gives a shit about him?"

"I do," Turner said. "If I'd listened to him in the first place, we might have some answers." He told them what he'd learned in the talks he'd had last night at the mission. "We need to follow up his movements that day, which probably means interviewing every homeless bum on the west side."

They divided that duty up by blocks, knowing they'd have to ask some of the beat cops to help.

"How about that nonmurder stuff?" Rodriguez asked.

"I'll be checking that today," Turner said.

Wilson said, "That friend of yours, Hume, the one with the

slouch fedora all the time, got interviewed by one of the national networks. He talked about an international conspiracy. If it keeps up, we're going to have a million reporters fucking things up."

Turner said, "We've got our cases to solve. We can deal with reporters if we have to."

At his desk Turner first began to organize the paperwork involved. They'd be buried in the shit up to their armpits even if they solved the whole thing today. A terrific breeze blew outside from the south. Unfortunately, the squad-room windows faced west. That earned them only an occasional puff of relief. Fenwick plugged the fan in. Someone on the night shift had left it on high. Before he could unplug it, papers flew. Fenwick swore, calling the squad on the night shift double and triple shits. When he got the fan under control, Turner could feel the breeze, but it barely kept up with the sweat that beaded on him from just sitting there. The weather reports predicted storms and more humidity.

He tried calling Jay Kendall, the columnist, who had been set up with a fake story. The reporter became suspicious and started pressing Turner for details and reasons for the call. After ten minutes of verbal fencing, Kendall admitted he had no idea who had set him up. "They covered their tracks completely. We haven't been able to figure out who owned the home they took me to in Springfield. The neighbors claim it's been vacant for years. State records show dummy corporations, and some of the title and deed background material is missing. We're still investigating."

He tried the chancery office for the bishop whose nude pictures were circulating. His cop status didn't get him past the receptionist. If he called back, he might be able to get through to the diocesan press-relations department.

After the phone calls Fenwick said, "I feel bad about what happened to Wilmer. If I'd been a little more patient . . ." He shrugged.

"We don't make perfect decisions," Turner said. "Who could

132

have said this time he knew something? I wish I'd listened more, but I'm not going to kick myself over it. It's done."

Fenwick said, "Yeah, you're right, I guess. What I want to know is, where was Wilmer going that day?"

"Ajax said 'a meeting with somebody.'"

"But who?" Fenwick asked. "Wilmer didn't tell Ajax?"

"No, but a reasonable guess is an appointment with the killers."

"How did he know them?" Fenwick asked.

"He saw something at Oak Street Beach," Turner guessed. "He was there."

"That's Lake Shore Drive area," Fenwick said. "They don't let the bums into that part of town, do they?"

"I know bums sleep on the benches in Lincoln Park. I've seen them early in the morning. Maybe he walked down from there. Think, Buck, if he didn't see it, how did he know the killers?" Turner asked. "Let's call back our witnesses and see if they remember seeing a bum."

They had the witnesses' home and work numbers. None of them remembered seeing anyone of Wilmer's description.

After those calls Fenwick suggested they go back to Wilmer's. "Maybe we missed something the first time."

Wind galed through the canyons of the city as they passed Sears Tower on Franklin, then turned west on Madison. "It's gonna be a hell of a storm when it hits," Fenwick said.

Turner said, "I wish it would make up its mind and get it the hell over with."

They entered Wilmer's building and trudged up the steps. Experienced cops, they had thoroughly inspected the space the day before. Still, they hunted over every inch. They even pulled back the tattered linoleum. Nothing. At one point Fenwick tried to open the window. "Double fuck," he swore when his heaving exertions produced no effect. He mopped his forehead with an enormous red-checked handkerchief. He said, "This is how I imagine hell. Close, hot, humid, no breeze." He glanced through the filthy window. He got a view of a mass of bricks two feet away. "No fire escape either. Crumbling brick makes a hell of an exterior decoration." He turned back to the room.

Turner stood in the doorway. He felt sweat drip from his armpits. "What was his life like?"

"Hell."

"No, I mean seriously. He showed up at the station constantly. He must have hung out down there a lot. It's not far, but it's a walk for an old drunk. Where else did he go?"

"The mission. The hospital. Any other place he felt like it in the city."

"I wonder if he went directly from the mission to his appointment."

"'Appointment' sounds like doctor shit to me," Fenwick said.

"Let's trace his path from the mission to the hospital." As they walked down the stairs, Turner said, "It's too hot in here. That's probably why he spent as many nights as he could at the mission. He couldn't sleep in this dump. Even if he was used to wearing all those clothes, the heat had to be impossible for him to sleep in."

As they got out of the car across the street from the mission, Fenwick said, "We are not really going to walk all the way from here to the hospital. Not in this heat."

"If he could do it, we can."

Fenwick grumbled but agreed.

After two blocks Fenwick said, "How do we know he took this way? Maybe he and a buddy grabbed a few snootfuls somewhere, or he took another direction for some side trip."

"Come on, Buck," Turner said. "It was hot that day. He'd take the most direct route. We can grab a cab back if you want, then try the other streets."

As they walked, they passed a few small businesses and numerous boarded-up shops as well as rubble-covered vacant lots, some still burned out from the riots in the sixties. In every business they stopped to ask if anyone knew Wilmer or had seen him that Saturday. Everybody they met, kids included, they asked about the old man. Their progress got slower and slower. Fortunately the neighborhood was essentially uninhabited. The westward movement of the Loop renovation wouldn't get here for a number of years yet.

When they got to Ashland Avenue, they turned north. Now the wind blew directly on their backs. The swirl of the gusts was almost enough to dry the sweat on their bodies. They'd long since shed their coats. Fenwick carried his draped over one arm. Turner slung his across his shoulder, hanging onto it with a finger under the collar.

Forty futile minutes later, they arrived at the hospital. It might have been a ten-minute walk from Madison, but their interviews had slowed them considerably. At the hospital they asked if someone could check the records to see if Wilmer had been in last Saturday.

It took fifteen air-conditioned minutes, which seemed to fly by, for them to get a negative answer.

Fenwick and Turner glanced at each other as they emerged in the miserable dampness outside.

"Didn't work," Turner said. "We should have called and asked."

"We had to try," Fenwick said. "Besides, I got some exercise."

It wasn't the first time in their partnership that one had gone along with an off chance the other suggested. As they walked back Turner said, "As long as the lieutenant is giving us as much manpower as we need right now, why don't we let the beat cops check all the other streets?"

Fenwick agreed. There were only a few streets that Wilmer could have taken between Madison and the hospital, but a team of men would be better than the two of them alone.

At the station Turner called back the chancery office. He got an official who claimed to know nothing of any pictures. The bishop was on his way to Rome for a long-planned vacation.

What Fenwick and Turner did next was paperwork. After a late lunch eaten at their desks, they waded into the mounds of forms and reports required by the department. They sat for three hours typing, grumbling, sweating, and drinking coffee.

Turner rubbed his eyes at five and sighed. "I'm not getting enough sleep," he told Fenwick.

"Worried about the kids?"

135

"Yeah, a little. The neighborhood is good, safe. Like last night with everybody calling the cops. Jeff at the hospital will be okay. Chasing after Brian and his friends the other night when his buddy's car broke down didn't help."

"Be glad they called you. They were scared to call the kid's dad, right? Brian and his friends trust you."

"Or at least I was the best parental alternative of the moment."

Fenwick said, "I envy your relationship with your kids. You're good at this parent shit."

Turner said, "I've got to take a break. I'm going to check in on Jeff. I'll be back in an hour or so."

"Take your time. All this shit will still be here."

Turner half hoped he'd run into Manfred at the hospital. He hadn't had time to call him. In Jeff's room he found his son napping, and Mrs. Talucci reading Descartes.

At seven he drove back toward the station. A massive thunderhead towered over the western horizon. He could see occasional flashes of lightning, but it was still too far away to hear the rumble of the storm. He hoped this meant a break in the weather.

His radio came to life at the corner of Grand and Halsted, near Goose Island, an old industrial district trying to make a comeback as a mixture of light industry, yuppies, and trendy shops. The dispatcher told him to get in touch with the station. He called and got hold of Fenwick.

His partner said, "Hurry back here. We've got a break in the old drunk's case."

Turner rushed through the streets. Varieties of trash swirled in the wind of the rising storm. Rushes of cool air burst through the open window of the un-air-conditioned car.

Fenwick jumped in the car as Turner pulled up to the station. "We got a tip," he said as he fastened his seat belt. "From another bum on the West Side."

"Anybody we're familiar with?"

"Name didn't ring a bell. He supposedly lives in the same building as Wilmer did."

"I thought it was uninhabited," Turner said. "We should have seen him or had some hint of his presence yesterday or this morning."

"They all run and hide when we come around. Supposedly he talked to your buddy Ajax and he knows something. While I was out grabbing something to eat, Ajax called. Asked for you. Didn't leave a number, but said it was urgent."

Turner hurried to Lake Street and headed west.

"Severe thunderstorm warning out," Fenwick said. "I think they got it right for once." Black clouds now filled the entire western horizon.

"Where are we supposed to meet this guy?" Turner asked.

"In the building, I guess. I didn't get the call. Somebody down at Eleventh and State did. I just got the message."

No one waited for them outside Wilmer's building. First they walked around the exterior. Brutal gusts of wind forced them to bend into the wind. No movement or light from inside gave any hint of current habitation.

"Let's check the place," Fenwick said. "We can start in Wilmer's room."

They entered, Fenwick carrying the flashlight. The natural gloom of the interior, combined with the gathering darkness, made it nearly impossible to see inside the building.

The old stairs creaked as they climbed to the top floor. As they reached the last step, Turner said, "Did I just hear something downstairs?" He looked over the banister and listened intently. The stairs climbed in such a way that he could see down to the ground floor.

"Just the weather," Fenwick said. "Let's hurry so we can get the hell out of here."

Lightening flashed and thunder rumbled as they reached the door to Wilmer's room. It was open. They'd left it closed that morning. For a moment they heard drops of rain tattoo on the roof sporadically, then with a rush the storm hit in earnest. Rain pounded on the roof. Seconds later drips began in the hallway.

"I don't like this." Turner had to shout over the roar of the rain and the crash of thunder, now almost continuous.

Fenwick shouted in return, "Fuck this shit. Let's look and get out." He shone the light through the doorway. They saw nothing. Fenwick pushed into the room cautiously. The flashes of light from the convulsion outside penetrated even through Wilmer's poor window and horrible view.

"What the fuck is that?" Fenwick pointed to a corner with a large mass that hadn't been there this morning.

They hurried forward. Fenwick held the light while Turner turned over the body.

"It's Ajax," Turner said. He looked up at Fenwick, was about to speak, when: "What was that?" he said.

Fenwick said, "I didn't hear anything."

"A door slammed. I'm sure of it."

"It was thunder," Fenwick said.

"I'm going to check," Turner said.

That light isn't right, Turner thought as he made his way down the hall to the top of the stairs. "Oh shit," he muttered. "Buck!" he yelled.

He didn't have to peer over the banister to know it was fire. He called the fire department on his radio as he looked carefully to see how far the blaze had gotten. Fenwick joined him.

"Triple fuck," Fenwick said.

"It's caught too much for us to get down," Turner said. The fire had already reached, or had been started on, the second floor. The movements of whoever started it had been covered by the rising storm.

"Rear exit," Turner said.

They rushed down the hall. Fire flashed up toward them from the back stairs, too.

"Fire escape," Fenwick said.

"Didn't see any as we walked around," Turner said.

"Triple fuck," Fenwick said.

They could feel the heat of the blaze now, different from the humidity. Sweat glistened on their faces.

They tried other doors on the floor. All but one opened. They broke that one in, but it too overlooked the street and a four-floor drop.

"Wilmer's room," Turner said.

"What?" Fenwick asked as they entered.

Turner hurried to the window. He tried to yank it up, with the same success Fenwick had had. Years of old paint and general disuse had closed it permanently. Turner wrapped his coat around his arm and smashed the glass. Some of the rotted wood fell away at the same time. Turner gazed up into the roaring storm. He ducked his head back in. Shadows of flames flickered in the doorway.

"We're going to walk up to the roof," Turner announced.

Fenwick stuck his head out. "Bullshit. We can't do that."

Turner reached through the window and touched the building opposite. He pulled his hand back in and said, "Both of these dumps are old brick with lots of crumbling spots. The space between isn't that big. Maybe two feet. We can crab walk it between the buildings."

"I'm too fat," Fenwick said. "What if I slip?"

"If one of us slips," Turner said, "then they scrape up flat cop from the pavement. In here we get charred corpses. We're taking the chance. It's only six feet or so to the roof."

Fenwick looked out. "Yeah, only."

"We don't have much time, Buck."

Fenwick said, "What do we do with the body? Drop him so he doesn't burn. He's already dead. Won't hurt him."

"If we get a chance, we can come back. Let's go." Turner gave his partner a shove.

Fenwick, an ultimately practical man, took one more look back and crawled onto the ledge. He turned back and said, "Go close the door to stop the smoke."

Turner hurried back, closed it, and returned to the window. He helped Fenwick gain balance. Fenwick wedged a foot in the brick wall two feet away. "Triple fuck." Rain sloshed off Fenwick's soaked body. He steadied his hands on each wall and immediately began to climb.

Moments later Turner followed. Wisps of smoke seeped under the door frame, following him out the window. Perhaps five minutes had passed since they discovered the body. Rain

139

poured onto Turner, soaking him instantly as he eased himself onto the sill and placed his left hand and foot on the building opposite. He grabbed the best holds he could. Thunder and lightning above and a four-floor drop below. He began his ascent. He moved one limb at a time, testing his grip as he moved. He barely heard Fenwick above him.

He dared to look up. He saw his friend with one arm gripped on the edge of Wilmer's building, his left foot wedged into a crevice on the building opposite. He scrabbled with the other foot, trying to catch a hold, and swung his left arm, trying to get it to join the right. Turner came up behind. He held on at three points, feet and left arm. He brought his right arm up. He saw Fenwick take another stab at swinging his weight for a grip. At that moment he shoved at Fenwick's butt. The last push put Fenwick onto the roof.

The shove unbalanced Turner. He clutched at the right wall and slipped; his knuckles scraped brick. Skin and blood mixed with the falling rain. He shouted in agony, but made his hand stab into the bricks.

"Grab hold," Fenwick called.

Turner looked up through the rain and saw Fenwick's hand two feet from him. Turner resumed inching his way up, ignoring his burning knuckles. Finally close enough, he reached for Fenwick's wrist. His partner grabbed at him. Their rain-slick hands rubbed against each other and missed. Turner felt himself unbalancing and beginning to tip. Fenwick's hand grabbed his wrist. For a second he felt a tug, then another slip, finally a firm grasp. For a second Turner dangled by only his friend's grip. Then he dug his feet into the bricks, launched himself upward, and with a heave from Fenwick made it to the top.

For a moment they sat breathing on the roof, listening to the wail of approaching fire engines. Temporarily safe, they sloshed through the puddles gathering on the roof, checking for a way down. Nothing. They studied the possibilities of climbing or jumping to the next building. Through dark and rain they couldn't see any. The building continued for another two stories of deteriorating brick. Rescue from the fire department was the only option.

By holding his hand up to his eyes to shield them from the rain, Turner got a spectacular view to the east of lightning striking and restriking the top of Sears Tower. By radio he told of their predicament, and a couple of minutes later a few shouts through the slowly abating storm caught the attention of the arriving firemen. The two policemen climbed down ladders to safety. Five minutes after they reached ground level, the roof caved in, and the departing storm helped douse the flames.

Two hours later Turner leaned back in his chair behind his desk at the station. In the locker room downstairs he'd changed from his sopping clothes. He wore gray gym shorts, white socks, gym shoes, and a white T-shirt with a Chicago police logo on it. Fenwick sat across from him in bright yellow Bermuda shorts and a flowered Hawaiian shirt, left in his locker from last year's squad picnic.

Wilson walked in and gave a wolf whistle. She stopped at Turner's desk, eyed his body appreciatively, ruffled his hair, and said, "I always forget you have the sexiest legs. At times I wish I wasn't quite so happily married."

"What about me?" Fenwick said.

Wilson said, "Buck, when you decide to trade in your size-twenty tent, we'll talk."

"What are you doing here?" Fenwick asked.

"Overtime, like you," Wilson said.

Carruthers burst into the room. "I heard on the radio. Is it true what happened to you guys?" He rushed across the room, eyes aglow and mouth agape.

Wilson asked, "What happened?"

The commander walked in, took one look at them and asked, "Do I want to hear this?"

Turner said, "I think this is the new uniform." He didn't remember feeling any fear until sitting down at his desk.

Thinking back on what almost happened, gave him a queasy feeling.

He and Buck explained to the assembled group about the fire and the dead body.

"Ajax was his real name?" Carruthers asked when they finished.

"Is that important?" Fenwick asked.

"You guys okay?" the commander asked.

"Good enough," Turner said.

Buck nodded agreement.

Wilson said, "They killed the old guy because he talked to you?"

"That doesn't make sense," the commander said. "He didn't tell you anything."

"Maybe they didn't know that," Turner said, "or they talked to him and found out he knew something that he hadn't told us yet, or they interrogated him about what Wilmer said, or maybe he bragged to someone about how in tight he was with the cops, or they simply wanted to kill us and he was bait, or I don't know. Buck said Ajax called and wanted to talk. Now we'll never know what he wanted to tell us."

Fenwick thumped his desk with his fist. "Double fuck. This shit doesn't make sense."

"Yeah, it does," Turner said. "To whoever's behind it, it makes perfect sense."

They discussed the murders and attacks for an hour, but got nowhere. The commander told them to give it a rest. They could start in the morning trying to trace Ajax's movements and figuring out why he'd died.

At home Turner found Brian and two of his buddies in the living room watching a video. For a couple of minutes Turner watched the Hollywood-style cops shoot guns and race around the streets smashing into corner fruit stands. He called the hospital to check on Jeff. The nurse told him his son was sleeping comfortably.

As soon as he hung up, the phone rang. He glanced at the clock. Nearly midnight. If it was one of Brian's friends, he'd strangle the kid.

Instead a disembodied voice said, "You were lucky; maybe your kids won't be. Leave your own alone." The phone clicked.

Immediately he called the official number to check on a trace. From a phone booth on the far north side of the city. Turner knew what the cops would find when they checked it out. Nothing, and no witnesses.

He tried to sleep. The boys downstairs had plans to stay the night and he heard their rough giggles and rustling for a while. He tossed restlessly. He was physically tired, but his mind raced, trying to figure out all the possibilities of the murders. The breeze had sprung up again, but still from the south, carrying more humidity. The front hadn't passed. Tonight's storm had been only a brief respite.

NINE

At seven thirty Friday morning Turner left for work early, warning Brain to be extra careful, and stopped to see Jeff. Paul found his son putting together a five-hundred-piece jigsaw puzzle. Jeff told him the doctor said he could go home tomorrow. Paul enjoyed a half hour with his son, then checked with building security. They assured him they could handle anything.

First thing at work Turner told Fenwick, between yawns, about last night's new threat.

When he finished, Fenwick said, "Every minority group in the country hates these people, but you were told to leave your own alone. The obvious conclusion is that the murder has to be gay-connected."

"I just don't buy it," Turner said.

"You trying to tell me gay people can't be murderers? They don't hate people who've tried to hurt them? They aren't capable of wanting revenge?"

"That's not what I'm saying. I just don't buy this big conspiracy theory."

"We have to investigate the possibility," Fenwick said.

Turner sighed. "You're right."

"Where do we begin?"

Turner said, "We talked to Nate Robeson and that didn't lead anywhere. According to the papers the most active radical crowd in the city these days is called FUCK-EM. Let's get Ian. He'll know where to start."

Turner called the *Gay Tribune* and then Ian's home phone. No one knew where he was or when he was expected. As one of the most noted gay reporters nationwide and one of the newspaper's oldest employees, Ian had a lot of freedom to come and go as he pleased. His roommate thought he might be being interviewed by national reporters, but she had no idea which ones.

An hour later Turner tossed his pen on a heap of forms and glared at the mounds of other paperwork on his desk. He picked up the phone and tried Ian again. Still no luck.

"Fuck this shit," Fenwick said, "let's nail down this Ajax character."

They drove to the West Side and the Mission of Eternal Peace, where they found the volunteers agog and energized from another late-night visit from the Reverend Mucklewrath.

They talked to Travis, the good-looking young volunteer Turner had met Wednesday. He looked as handsome as he had two days ago, but more haggard. Travis explained that he'd traded shifts that day with a buddy. He yawned at them. "I'm a little tired, working two shifts in a row, but he does me favors so I return them. Besides, the reverend was here." A faint rosy afterglow appeared on his cheeks.

Turner sympathized with the lack of sleep. He told Travis about Ajax.

"He's dead?" Travis said, once again sounding genuinely shocked as he had the other night. He shook his head. "Ajax, for all of his faults, was one of the better ones we dealt with. He seemed to have a little class in his background, you know?"

"Did he come in last night?"

"Ajax checked in, but he left. He didn't even finish his job. Ajax is fairly unreliable, but he usually tells somebody he's going." The kid smiled briefly. "In fact, he usually makes a stink about it, claiming he strained a muscle and he has to run to the doctor or something. It's usually some dumb excuse."

"You sure he didn't tell anybody?"

"You can come back tonight and ask, but I doubt it."

"How did he seem last night?" Turner said.

"I'm not sure I remember. We got pretty crowded because of the rain. I remember assigning him his task. I didn't know he was gone until one of the custodians found Ajax's mop and pail and reported them abandoned. No one got excited. One of them taking off like that is not all that rare an occurrence."

"Did he have any fairly permanent or even a favorite place to stay?" Fenwick asked.

"Not that I know of."

Early that day the police districts in the area had been notified of Ajax's death; they would inform all the cops at their morning roll calls to ask every homeless person they could for any information about him. On rare occasions this method produced a helpful clue.

Turner and Fenwick stopped at the fire scene at Wilmer's. Investigators from the fire department shifted rubble and debris. The torrential rain the night before hadn't checked the fire until the building was almost completely destroyed.

The cops introduced themselves to one of the investigators.

"You the guys we rescued last night?" she asked.

They nodded.

She shook her head. "You guys were lucky. This was arson and the place was supposed to go fast. The stairway did, but this place was built years ago. The plaster walls held it up long enough."

Fenwick said, "I'll light a candle to the masons from the last century."

Turner asked, "Did you find the body?"

"What was left of it. You won't be able to find out much from what we got. We call them crispy critters." Like cops, medical examiners, and most people who dealt with the remnants of human life, she had a bizarre sense of humor.

"Anything at all to tell about who did it or how?" Fenwick asked.

"Didn't take a rocket scientist. Found a couple of charred standard-issue gasoline cans they left behind. You pour the gasoline and light a match. Not much to it."

"I wish we could have saved the body," Turner said.

"No chance," the investigator said. "You spend a couple of minutes tossing a dead body around and you're as dead as he is. Who does that help?"

On the way back to Area Ten headquarters, they stopped by the Twelfth District police station. It was on their way, and Wilmer and many of the homeless lived within the district's boundaries. They asked to talk to any of the beat cops who knew Ajax, or where he hung out, or who his friends were.

Immediately after they explained their needs, a gray-haired cop behind the desk said, "I know exactly the guy you want. He's out for now; let me get him in here for you." He notified the watch commander and then, using the intercom on the back wall, he called a car into the station.

Five minutes later Dwight Perez stumped up the stairs. He greeted the detectives, and when they told him what they needed, he said, "No problem. I know all these guys."

They walked through the midday heat to the Palace Grill. On the way Dwight gave them far more of his life history than they would ever have cared to know. As they seated themselves on stools at the counter near the back Perez said, "I got this shit detail. I arrest too many people for minor crap. They don't tell me that, but I figured it out: I got to learn, I got to get myself under control. So, I do the bums. I know everything you need to know. What do you want?"

"You know an Ajax?" Fenwick asked.

"Sure. The old guy who died in the fire. Never had a permanent place to stay. Claimed to have been in the navy in World War II. Seemed an okay enough guy. What's the deal with him? Why you guys interested?"

"Why didn't you respond to this morning's announcement about him?" Fenwick asked.

147

"I didn't hear one. I sat in the back like usual trying to get some paperwork done."

"We think he may have been killed because of what he knew in a murder investigation, or what the killer thought he knew."

"No shit. Old Ajax? I wouldn't rely too much on what any of these old guys told you."

"We don't have much choice," Fenwick said. "We haven't got much to go on." He explained about the murders. "We're trying to trace his movements last night," Fenwick finished.

"I didn't know Wilmer. He didn't like me. Avoided me. About Ajax, did you try the Mission of Eternal Peace?"

"Yeah," Turner said.

Perez said, "Those guys are a little religious for my taste, but they do a great job with these people."

"Where would he go, and why would he leave a place where his meal and bed were set for the night?" Turner asked.

"He'd leave for money, booze, cigarettes, an argument, almost anything. You can't tell with these people."

"Where would he go?"

"Hard to tell, but a lot of them have a sort of meeting house of their own, down on Harrison west of Ashland. It's an old place, kind of wedged between a bunch of old buildings and the expressway. You might try there."

He gave them the location. Turner and Fenwick drove over. They knocked on the doors of several buildings they thought were the right ones. No one answered. All of the buildings looked abandoned and totally unused. They walked around to the alley. They could see and hear the rush of traffic on the Eisenhower Expressway just below them. In the alley behind the fourth building, they saw what looked like the clubhouse you tried to put together in your back yard when you were a kid, only worse. The hut seemed held together by shadows and rusty nails.

A woman, who looked to be at least in her nineties, sat on what would generously be called a front stoop. A cigarette dangled from the left side of her mouth, smoke curling into the morning haze. The torn and shabby sleeves of her dress hung oddly, one ripped off near the shoulder, the other dangling to the elbow. The dress covered her spraddled legs to the ankle.

They introduced themselves and showed their stars. The ends of her mouth moved up microscopically in what might have been meant to be a smile.

Turner said, "Ma'am, we're looking for anybody who knew a gentleman named Ajax."

"You looking for a gentleman, you came to the wrong place. You want a bum, you come to the right place." She puffed placidly on her cigarette. A pack sat by her knee. A mound of butts sat between her bare feet.

"Yes, ma'am," Turner said. "I misspoke. Could you help us? We need to speak to anyone who knew him."

The microscopic maybe-smile came and went. She said, "I'm here most of the time. He ain't here now."

"No, ma'am. We're sorry to say, especially if he was a friend of yours, he's dead."

She took a long drag on her cigarette. Her aged spotted hands moved in circles over the folds of her dress. Just before the ash would have dropped in her lap, she flicked the butt toward the street, missing Fenwick by an inch.

"Wasn't a bad old guy," she said. "What got him? Booze, loneliness, or he just get tired of living?"

"He was murdered last night," Fenwick said. "We're trying to trace his movements. If you're here a lot of the time, maybe you saw him last night."

"I may have, but you need to make it worth my while."

Turner had never given cash to an informant. In his experience police work didn't happen that way.

Fenwick said, "We'll get you a pack of cigarettes."

She spat on the ground at his feet. "Try again, sonny."

"A carton, and that's it," Fenwick said.

"I get the carton, I talk."

Turner said, "No talk, no cigarettes."

The enigmatic smile again. She was sort of an aging Mona Lisa, sitting on an urban dung heap.

She lit another cigarette, pointed to Turner, and said, "You, I

149

trust." She took a lung-destroying drag on her cigarette. "Okay, he came in last night all excited. Said he'd finally made it to easy street. Said he had friends now, who'd take care of him. I laughed at him. Everybody around here says the same thing when they score a bottle or get some idiot to hand them a quarter."

She dragged on the cigarette, blew a smoke ring.

"He didn't say who it was?" Fenwick asked.

"Nope."

"Or where he was going?"

"Nope."

"Do you remember anything else about what he said?" Turner asked.

"Only what I told you."

"When did he leave?"

"Before the storm. I remember that." She paused and thought a minute while taking several puffs on her cigarette.

"Did he say where he was going?" Turner asked.

"Nope. Don't think he said. I know I don't remember. When do I get my cigarettes?"

"Couple more questions," Turner said. "Did he have any friends here? Someone that he'd confide in or that he was close to."

"No friends here," she said. "No relationships. We barely give each other our names. It's safe here and anonymous. Some of us have pasts to hide from."

After Turner finished a few more questions he said to her, "We'll be back."

He made Fenwick stop at a rundown corner drugstore. They dropped off the cigarettes. Back at their desks in the station Turner said to Fenwick, "I think she liked you. I think she winked at you several times."

"That why she threw cigarette butts at me and spat at me?" Fenwick asked.

"She was showing you her affection and regard."

"We got a lot of nothing again from all this running around. We spent money for a carton of cigarettes, and she didn't know shit. Why couldn't we have a nice domestic? A little blood on the kitchen floor, the husband or wife with a bloody knife and sobbing their eyes out, waiting for us to get there so they can confess?"

Fenwick picked up an incoming call, mumbled a few words and hung up. "That was one of Mucklewrath's people. The good reverend would like to see us." He turned to Wilson, "Is he still using his kid's ashes in the act?"

Wilson said, "Yeah. They line up to get healed, and they have to walk past the urn with the ashes. They've got these American flag–draped bins that people throw money in, and I mean green stuff. None of this coin shit. The urn sits on a table with a big American flag draped over it."

Fenwick said, "That is such shit."

"Let's go see what he wants," Turner said.

Before they left, Turner tried Ian again. No luck.

The good reverend had left instructions at the hotel for them to meet him at Soldier Field. They maneuvered through traffic to the stadium.

They found the reverend on the football field near the south end, about ten feet from his daughter's urn.

He greeted them with grave solemnity then said, "I have a few problems, gentlemen. I need to leave this city, and your investigation isn't done. What do you intend to do about it?"

Turner said, "You're free to go, if that's what's bothering you."

"I assumed I was. I want the killers found and executed. I see news reports, and police officials make announcements, but I see no action."

Both cops said nothing.

He berated them for about five minutes for cop inefficiency. They took it stolidly.

Finally, the reverend paused dramatically, drew a deep breath, and leaning one hand on his daughter's urn said, "I'm scared."

"Of what?" Turner said.

Mucklewrath talked about his empire, his contributions, his university, his followers, his senatorial duties.

He wound down again and Fenwick asked, "What are you afraid of?"

Mucklewrath paused, stared dramatically into the distance as if reading God's pronouncements through the humidity and haze. Finally his gaze returned to earth. Turner watched as the man's shoulders sagged and the face crumpled nearly to tears. He said, "Son, I'm afraid of losing it all."

"Who could make that happen?" Turner asked.

He dug in his pocket and brought out a crumpled piece of paper. "Someone placed this on the pedestal where I put the urn with my daughter's ashes. I found it when I arrived this morning."

Turner took the 8½-by-11 piece of paper and examined it. Fenwick looked over his shoulder.

The writing said, "Obviously, you aren't sorry enough."

They turned from the note to the reverend.

He said, "I've lost the most precious person in the whole world, but there are others I love deeply. I can't bear to see any more of them hurt. I can't let this kind of thing happen." His silken voice whispered, "Gentlemen, this must stop."

"Any of your people around here who could have done this?" Turner asked.

The reverend shook his head. "They don't come until three hours before opening. The park district must be around, and the local security."

"Could someone in your organization do this?" Turner asked.

"A few days ago, I thought not. Now, I'm not so sure. I don't know any one specifically. I can't let anything like what happened to Chistina happen again."

"We'll talk to the men on duty, Reverend," Turner said.

The reverend didn't seem to have an ounce of bombast left. He said, "Please, do anything you can."

They found the head of security, who helped them organize questioning of the guards from the day shift. He told them, "I can vouch for the fact that the note was not there when I came on duty or when these people started this morning. I check the entire stadium myself. I walk around every inch of the place. It wasn't there. I've questioned all of my people. Nobody admits anything. You're welcome to try."

They spent an hour and a half questioning the members of the security team. They got the same amount of information as the head of security did: none.

They took a list of all the employees in the stadium at the time, including a list of those working with the Mucklewrath group.

Back at the station they ran the names through the computer for quick background checks on all of them. The computer showed nothing.

Around one Fenwick bashed his hand down on his computer console. "One of the people we talked to at Soldier Field knows the whole operation we've been dealing with." He bashed the computer top again. "One of those double shits lied to us."

Fenwick rarely got to the bashing stage. Years ago Turner had seen him put his foot through a TV screen after he'd found two dead kids and a little baby so mutilated by abusive parents it only lived a few hours.

Turner leaned back in his chair and rubbed his hands across his eyes. "We're driving ourselves nuts with this. We've missed something."

Fenwick looked up at him. They listened to Carruthers typing madly on a report, probably days if not weeks overdue.

Turned tried the paper again. They caught Ian just as he got in. He'd been doing interviews all morning for national news shows and setting up appearances, as he put it, on Oprah, Phil, Joan, and Sally. Turner explained what they needed. With some reluctance, Ian agreed. Before leaving, Turner called Brian and Jeff. Everything was quiet with them. Jeff told him Dr. Manfred had stopped by and had promised to stop in again this evening.

Turner and Fenwick caught a weather report before leaving the station. Severe thunderstorm warnings were in effect for most of northern Illinois, the southern half of Wisconsin, and northwest Indiana. For the moment the humidity held and barely a breath of wind stirred.

They met Ian at the corner of Clark and Montrose, near the

153

newspaper office. The large reporter climbed into the back of their unmarked car. He wore his slouch fedora even in the car, although the smallest bump caused the crown to hit the roof. Turner gave him full details.

Ian nodded. "You're right about talking to FUCK-EM, although I don't see them as killers. A lot of noise and protest, even a little violence, but not murder."

"It's a start," Turner said. "One thing, they've got a large-enough organization so that they could field enough people to plan and carry out all these crimes."

"It might be a little difficult finding them at this hour of the day," Ian said, "but we can try a few of their usual haunts." He told them the leader of the group was a Bruce Davidson, a student at the University of Chicago.

Following Ian's directions they stopped at various places the FUCK-EM group met or hung around. The third place was a cabaret-bar in the basement of a closed department store at the corner of Lincoln and Belmont. They walked down a narrow flight of stairs to a room kept luridly dark to the point of absurdity.

Peering around in the dimness, Fenwick asked, "Is this a gay bar?"

Ian said, "No, it's mostly straight and very trendy, always jammed at night."

After their eyes adjusted, they found Bruce Davidson haranguing several cronies, one of them Rusty the hustler.

They showed their stars to the bartender, who turned out to be the owner. He offered them drinks. Fenwick and Turner took coffee. Ian accepted a beer.

The intent group barely looked up even when the three stood above their booth. Rusty sneered at Turner and said, "Who's the beefy buddy?"

They showed their stars. Rusty began to get nasty, but the owner said, "Shut the fuck up. I don't want no trouble in here. I'll throw him out."

"We just want to talk with Bruce for now," Fenwick said, "but nobody leaves."

The owner led the others away.

After he sat in the booth, Turner discovered a possible reason for the excessive dimness. What Turner, who grew up in the city, would have called jungle rot covered nine tenths of the wall surface. He touched it with a fingertip. A five-inch piece of jagged plaster fell to the floor. He tried to rub the green stain on his fingertip on a napkin from the metal container on the table. No luck. He kept his left side a safe distance from the wall.

"What's this all about, Ian?" Bruce asked. He wore a black T-shirt, black 501's, a necklace made of leather thongs, four earrings going up the side of one ear, and lace up black leather boots. Bruce slumped in his seat against the wall. He was either unaware of or didn't care about the creeping filth his side rested against. Turner guessed that if he was over the age of twenty-one, his birthday had been yesterday.

Ian said, "It's about all the shit that's been happening to the straight people."

"And about the possibility of Donald Mucklewrath being gay," Turner added.

"Why come talk to me?"

Turner said, "You're the head of FUCK-EM, and your group has been involved in outing people and in violent protests."

"Why should I talk to cops? Last time we had a demonstration you beat up half our members."

Ian said, "Half your members had camped out in Buckingham Fountain. Besides your skins getting terminally wrinkled, little old ladies began to be upset when you took to relieving yourselves in the water."

Bruce looked sheepish. He still sported prominent zits on his nose. He said, "Well, the planning on that could have been a little better, but the police should have been more gentle dragging us out."

Turner didn't want a full-scale discussion of police tactics.

Ian said, "Bruce, remember it's me you're talking to. The one who knows everybody's dirty little secrets, including yours. I've helped you out of a couple of tight jams." He didn't explain to the cops what secrets and jams. Turner wasn't sure he wanted to know. "You owe me several big ones. I'd appreciate it if you'd answer their questions."

Bruce squirmed and gave the cops a wary look, but he nodded. "I'll do what I can."

Turner said, "First tell us about Donald Mucklewrath."

"What's to tell? We heard he was gay, then we got a confirmation."

"From Rusty," Turner said.

"How'd you know?" Davidson said.

"A good source."

"If Donald is gay, we're going to make that two-bit bastard and his asshole father pay, but we never had a meeting with him. He never returns our calls."

Switching topics, Turner explained why they thought someone in the gay community might be behind the pranks and perhaps the murders.

"They threatened you? You're a gay cop? And they know? And you've got kids?"

"Yes," Turner said.

"Wow."

Turner asked, "Have you heard of any kind of plot like this in the community?"

"No," Bruce said. "We're an activist group for gay rights and more help for people with AIDS, but we don't do that kind of shit. We believe in creative nonviolence."

"What the hell does that mean?" Fenwick asked.

Bruce had the grace to blush. "I'm not sure. I guess it means, we want to push people around and we hope they don't push back."

"How about members of the group who would want to go beyond creativity? You got any hotheads who might act on their own?" Turner asked.

"They're all talkers," Davidson said. "The most vocal ones are the ones who can't organize for shit. They want to be politically correct. The rest of us want action."

"Who are some of the most politically correct ones?" Turner said.

Bruce shrugged.

Ian said, "Come on, Bruce."

"Rusty, for one," Bruce said. "Nobody else, really. We're pretty radical, but in the beginning some people were really nuts. The more vocal ones usually just drop out after a meeting or two. Rusty's stayed a lot longer than any others."

"How about any other person or group in the community?" Turner asked.

"Well, you always hear talk about what people would like to do to bigoted straights. It doesn't mean anything. Every gay person does it. You know, get revenge, get the oppressor. Couple guys I knew who tested positive swore they'd get even with members of the FDA who didn't approve drugs fast enough. They got too sick and weak to do anything about it. They died a couple months ago." Davidson rotated his empty beer glass between his fingers as he talked.

Ian said, "Paul, you'd have to arrest yourself and most of the rest of the gay community if you wanted all the people who'd ever wished nasty things to happen to bigoted straights."

Turner shrugged. "Any rumor in the community of any kind?" he asked. "The smallest hint of any person in the group who might turn to violence?"

Bruce shook his head.

After a few more minutes of fruitless questions and useless answers, Turner said, "Let's try Rusty."

Rusty took Bruce's place in the corner of the booth. Ian sat next to him, Turner and Fenwick opposite.

Rusty slumped even more tightly than his friend against the wall. Turner saw green stains on the back of the shoulder strap of his tank top.

"I told you the other night I'm only talking with a lawyer present."

Ian said, "But I'm not a cop, and I'm willing to beat the shit out of your arrogant ass."

"He threatened me," Rusty said. "You both heard him. He can't do that. You have to stop him."

Fenwick said, "We don't have to do shit."

157

"I'll call for help," Rusty said.

"We are the police," Fenwick pointed out.

"Shit," Rusty said. "I'm leaving." He looked at Ian and even tried a brief shove.

Ian simply let his six-foot-six frame respond to the push as if it came from a playful cat.

Rusty looked around wildly. No possibility of the U.S. cavalry racing to the rescue. At the far end of the room the owner ignored them, keeping himself busy with his bartending duties. Anger and frustration nearly brought tears to the hardened hustler's face.

Turner said, "Look, Rusty. We don't mean you any harm. We don't want to bust you. We just need any help we can get in solving the murders."

"But I don't know anything," Rusty said.

His voice grated on Turner, a teenage whine reminiscent of Brian at his worst.

"Just a few questions," Turner said.

Rusty crossed his arms over his chest and set his lips in a firm line. If he'd been a fifty-year-old madam with tons of makeup, he might have made the cool defiance he wanted to portray work. As it was, he looked like a petulant little brat.

Turner said, "You're pretty serious about FUCK-EM and what they stand for."

"You would be too, if you weren't a fucking cop, a traitor to your own people."

Fenwick asked, "How do you justify being a hustler and being an activist?"

Rusty snorted at him. "You don't know shit. I'll rip off the world any way I can. I'll especially screw anybody who's antigay and make them pay for it. That's why I got Do—"

"That's how you stumbled onto Donald Mucklewrath," Turner finished for him.

"I didn't say that," Rusty said.

"Give it a rest," Turner said. "We know you're the one who turned him over to the outing crowd. Gill Garret told us Tuesday. Where'd you meet Mucklewrath?"

"I said all I'm going to say," Rusty said.

"Let's take him down to the station and book him," Fenwick said.

Turner recognized the tactic instantly; unfortunately Rusty did too. The kid sneered. "Arrest me for what? And don't try playing good cop, bad cop with me. It won't work."

Fenwick let irritation creep into his voice as he said, "You little prick. You might think you're a lawyer, but you don't know shit."

Rusty turned to Ian. "You heard a cop threaten me. Aren't you going to make that into a headline in your paper?"

"It's not my paper," Ian said. "I'm only a reporter and you're an uppity little creep. Now answer the man's questions."

They got the story out of him, along with a great deal of unattractive whining and complaining. He'd met Donald Mucklewrath at a very high-class businessmen's dinner party given in a Lake Forest mansion. One of the businessmen thought it would be a lot of fun to bring Rusty and say he was his nephew from out of town. Rusty thought it was a stupid idea, but the man was a faithful, well-paying customer, so he went. He'd run into Mucklewrath coming out of the john. One thing led to another and by the end of the evening Rusty had another customer. From one of the other guests at the party, Rusty found out his conquest was Donald Mucklewrath. He'd hardly been able to contain his glee. They'd gone to bed a week later and Rusty'd reported this to FUCK-EM.

"I didn't know anything about the meeting with Mucklewrath to out him. The rest of them do that kind of stuff. They don't trust me because I have a temper."

Minutes later they left, learning nothing else new.

They dropped Ian off back at the paper. Fenwick drove back toward the station. "Now what?" he said.

"I'm not sure what else there is to check," Turner said. "We've interviewed several zillion people, all of whom know nothing. All we've got are the victims. I thought the outing angle would get us somewhere, and we don't know anything

159

more about the Mucklewrath family based on the Donald-is-gay rumor." He shrugged.

For several minutes they rode in silence down Halsted Street. At Chicago Avenue Fenwick said, "I wonder how Wilmer got the virus."

"What do you mean?"

"He's an old guy and not attractive. The report said he wasn't an addict. I didn't see anything in the medical report about a blood transfusion. So who would have sex with him?"

Turner said, "A mystery we'll probably never solve."

Occasional bursts of wind stirred the air as they ran into a late afternoon traffic snarl in Greektown. While they waited for the light at Jackson and Halsted, Fenwick said, "Where could Wilmer meet somebody? Any bar he went in, would throw him out. You told me Ajax said he wasn't part of any group."

"At the hospital?" Turner guessed.

"Maybe he had a close friend, or lover, or fuck buddy there," Fenwick said. "Maybe that person would know about Wilmer's movements that day or what he knew."

"We had that with Ajax, I thought," Turner said.

"It's an idea."

Turner said, "We only talked to the eight-to-four shift at the hospital. We should have gotten back to them before this."

"I can't today," Fenwick said. "I gotta get home. I promised to take the girls for doctor's appointments. Madge can't be home."

"Nothing wrong with the girls?"

"No, regular stuff, but I have to do it. Madge's been ragging at me lately with all this overtime. If I thought we'd actually learn something, I'd go with you."

"No problem. I'll handle it. I'm sure you're right. It'll be another dead end."

Before driving to City Hospital Turner stopped at home. At four o'clock Brian was downstairs playing Nintendo with some buddies. Turner spotted the patrol car outside. He waved to the cops keeping watch. They wouldn't be able to keep a patrol car by his home indefinitely.

He listened to the radio on the way over and heard that beyond a severe thunderstorm warning, a tornado watch had been posted for the Chicago area. For now, the muggy air stirred restlessly, with occasional gusts of wind attacking more vigorously. As he walked from the parking lot into the hospital, he observed unpleasantly black clouds filling the western horizon.

In the AIDS ward he found a nurse who looked to be about nineteen, all pink in good health. He explained why he'd come. "I really guess I don't expect to find anything, but I thought I'd give it a try."

"No problem," she said. "It's quiet right now on the floor. Let me get anybody who's around. You can ask all of us at the same time."

Minutes later she assembled four people at the nurses' station. All of them remembered Wilmer.

After getting introductions and pleasantries out of the way, Turner asked, "Did he have any good friends?"

Three shook their heads no. The fourth said, "I saw him most often." His name was Tommy Smith, about twenty-five with the lightest blond hair Turner had ever seen. "He always teased me about being young and attractive. I've got a wife and two kids. I'm as straight as they come, but I let the old guy tease and have his fun. He tried to pinch my ass a couple times, but he stopped after I had a firm talk with him. He always asked for me. Anyway, I guess his best buddy was that Dr. Manfred who deals with lots of the people with AIDS."

"Was he a member of any of the AIDS support groups?" Turner asked.

"No. He was an independent old guy. I admired that."

"How about friends, anybody he might share confidences with?"

The twenty-five-year-old said, "He always did one odd thing, I thought. He'd visit the sickest person with AIDS who was in the hospital. Or at any rate he tried to. Wilmer wasn't the

161

prettiest visitor for people, and some of the families tried to drive him away, but the abandoned ones, people whose families wouldn't accept that they were gay or that they were dying, those are the ones he visited. They liked his visits. I never got any complaints."

"Anybody he talked to more than others?" Turner asked.

Smith shrugged. "Most of the ones he visited are dead. He'd sit with them for hours and read, or listen to them. Wilmer always talked my ear off. It surprised me that he listened to them so well."

The other nursing staff had drifted off one by one during this conversation. Tommy Smith said, "I guess the one who's still alive that he talked to most was old Mr. Gravelstone. I didn't see him here the other day. I thought he died. At the end of my shift yesterday, I found out he'd improved enough to be sent home on Monday afternoon." Smith gave him the address, an apartment in Calumet Park, a south suburb just outside the city.

"You know, a couple of people asked the same questions you just did about Wilmer this week. Who he knew and talked to."

"Who asked?" Turner asked.

"One was a phone call. Said he was a member of the family trying to set up funeral arrangements. Wanted to be sure everybody knew about it."

"He leave a name?"

Tommy Smith thought a minute. "No, said he was with some mortuary. I don't remember which one. Funny he didn't say."

"What did you tell him?"

"I told him everybody knew about it, because, like I said, I thought Mr. Gravelstone died. We lose so many of them."

"Who else wanted to know?" Turner asked.

"Dr. Manfred," Smith said.

T E N

Turner's mind whirled around the name Manfred. He tried to keep his attraction for the man out of his thinking. Before leaving the hospital, he tried calling the doctor's answering service. They told him that Manfred was unavailable, that he might call in later if Turner wanted to leave a message. He decided against this. If his suspicions proved groundless, he'd feel like a fool.

Turner remembered the doctor's warmth and caring, the stirring of desire when they embraced. He tried to put another interpretation on the nurse's words, and found enough innocent ones to satisfy him for the moment. Many people had told him of the doctor's great caring and thorough concern for his patients and their loved ones. This connection to Wilmer had to be the same thing.

Turner saw the storm before he reached the electronically activated doors. The trees that lined the parking lot bent double with the gusts of wind. Sheets of rain blew in waves over the parking lot. Claps of thunder, followed ten or more seconds later by crashes of lightning, told Turner in the folklore he'd learned as a kid that the center of the storm had a ways to come. He dashed through the storm to his car.

Turner tossed his drenched sport coat into the back seat. He debated visiting Gravelstone that night. The witness probably wouldn't know anything. The rain would tie up traffic miserably on all the rush-hour-clogged expressways, but his suspicion of Manfred nagged at him. He'd give it a try. He had to know the truth.

Turner entered the Dan Ryan at Roosevelt Road, and was immediately sorry he'd decided to go. Bad weather screwed up traffic; a major storm snarled it hopelessly. He almost gave up driving to the end of the city, but it would be one less thing to do tomorrow, and they were already up to their nipples in paper work. Maybe it would be a brief shower. This turned into a false hope. As Turner inched his way south, the storm increased in intensity. His windshield wipers, on fast, barely kept up with the sluicing downpour. On occasion the viaducts on the expressways in the city filled with water after an intense rain. If they did, his drive back home could turn into a major adventure.

An hour and fifteen minutes later, nerves frayed, exhausted from his lack of sleep in the past few days, Turner took the 127th Street exit. As he waited for the light to change at the corner at the top of the ramp, the radio weatherman informed him the National Weather Service had just issued tornado warnings for the entire metropolitan area. Numerous funnels had been sighted fifty miles west of the city.

He drove four blocks and almost missed his turn because he couldn't see the street sign through the downpour. He turned right up Lincoln Avenue and drove three blocks. Just before the road ended in a clump of underbrush and trees, he found the apartment building. Through the rain he could see many of the outside lights broken. Crumbling bricks and cracked cement formed an outer perimeter of decay. Lights filtered out of numerous apartments. Some had only sheets covering the picture windows, through which he could discern the yellow of a lamp gleam or the blue of the TV screen.

He fought the urge to go home. He'd come this far, he might as well stick it out.

164

A small parking lot sat between two identical apartment buildings. He pulled in and found a slot second from the end, then stayed in the car a minute listening to the rain pound on the roof and watching it rush off the second-story balcony of the apartments. Wishing for the millionth time that he'd bought an umbrella to leave in the car for just such occasions, he grabbed the door handle, yanked up, tossed the door open, threw himself out, slammed the door, and ran to the shelter of the overhang. The number he wanted, twenty-eight, was on the second floor, necessitating a dash up two flights of stairs tacked onto the end of the building and open to the unfriendly elements. His jacket still lying soaked in the back of the car, he dashed up the stairs in his white shirt and tie. What the rain hadn't plastered to his skin in the brief dash from the car, this new venture into the elements finished.

This has got to be one of the dumber things I've done in a while, Turner thought as he tapped at the door to number twenty-eight. No answer. He knocked harder, thought of giving it a good solid pound or two when he heard a feeble voice, barely audible over the crash and bash of the storm.

He put his ear to the door, waited for a respite from the thunder, and knocked again. He definitely heard the voice this time. After a brief hesitation, he turned the knob. The door opened and he entered.

A gust of wind nearly blew the door out of his hand. Black and stormy as it was outside, it was almost better than inside the apartment.

He saw an old man in the middle of a bed that took up two thirds of the tiny room. "Who?" the man on the bed asked. His voice rattled wheezily.

Turner shut the door and said into the relative quiet, "A friend. I'm a police office." His eyes took a moment to adjust to the total dark. A glow of light from the few fixtures around the building penetrated through the thin sheet over the window to give off some light. The flashes of lightning provided more.

The old man barely flickered a nod at him.

"Is there a light?" Turner asked.

The old man raised a finger off the bed to point toward a shelf several feet above him and to the left. Turner inched his way toward it, unsure of what might be on the floor. On the shelf, by feel and by waiting for a lightning flash, he found the stubs of several candles. Next to them he found a pack of matches.

He lit the candle. Its flickers barely added to that provided by the lightning, and nature's display brought far more illumination to the room. At least now Turner could see with some degree of consistency.

The shelf divided the apartment. He stood now in a combination livingroom–bedroom. The other side of the shelf contained a narrow kitchen, with a stove but no refrigerator. Two glasses, a plate, and a spoon rested unwashed on the narrow cupboard. A door off this to the right led to a tiny bathroom. The only furniture in the apartment was the bed. He eased himself down onto it, placed the candle carefully on the arm of the sofa.

The old man said, "You shouldn't get close. I have AIDS."

Turner took the wrinkled and roughened hand and held it. He said, "Mr. Gravelstone, I want to make sure you understand. I have some questions to ask."

Gravelstone nodded. Turner detected no fear in the eyes he saw in the dim light. He noted a fevered intensity, yet he thought he saw a calm serenity underneath.

Gravelstone mumbled something.

Turner placed his ear close to the old man's mouth. "I want to sit up," Gravelstone gasped.

Turner helped him, then asked, "How can they let you be at home when you're this sick?"

Gravelstone tried a smile. When he talked, he whispered and often had to pause to draw a deep breath. "I'm better off here. All my possessions are gone, but it's still my home. I've lived here thirty years. It's my own room, in my own home, such as it is." The old man asked for water. Turner washed one of the glasses in the kitchen, filled it, and brought it to him.

The room felt close and humid. Turner's shirt clung uncomfortably to his torso. He loosened his tie and unbuttoned the top two buttons for a little comfort. The apartment smelled of must and mildew.

Turner made certain Gravelstone was comfortable, then asked, "You understand I'm from the police?"

Gravelstone nodded.

"I want to ask you some questions."

Gravelstone's eyes didn't leave Turner's face for an instant. Oddly, Turner found the stare almost comforting. It was the most alive part of the human being he now sat with.

"Go ahead," Gravelstone whispered.

"I'm here about Wilmer Pinsakowski."

Gravelstone did not seem startled.

"You know he's dead?"

"Young man," he wheezed, "perhaps you'd better let me tell you the story."

Turner nodded.

"I was a priest years ago in another city," the old man began. Frequently his coughs and wheezes interrupted his speech. Turner refilled the water glass and helped him sip from it when the old man indicated a need. "The church threw me out. It was awful. One of my parishioners hated me. She accused me of molesting her daughter. It was a lie, a vicious untruth. Somehow word got out and it made a hideous scandal. I always thought it was the pastor of my last parish. He was a vicious piece of hypocritical shit." He breathed deeply for several minutes until the sting of the memory eased. "My friends turned their backs. The parish, the diocese, the whole community went crazy. An innocent man hounded from his real home.

"I came here. No bishop anywhere would let me be a priest in his diocese. For thirty years I've suffered. I've come to hate the Catholic church for its cruelty to me." He gasped and Turner helped him to more water. Gravelstone continued, "I hate straight people. I joined the conspiracy gladly."

Turner leaned closer.

"Unfortunately," he wheezed, "we didn't all agree. A few of us wanted to use violence and death to show them their evil ways: holding up AIDS funding, keeping it too little, stopping legislation against gay-bashing." He gasped for breath for several minutes, his emotions outrunning his body's ability to cope. He resumed, "So we fought and planned, and no one said a word to anyone outside the group." He sighed deeply. "Except me."

"What did you plan?" Turner asked.

"Revenge. Against anyone who ever hurt gay people. Against the stupid, ignorant bigots who feed on hate. We would make them sorry. I wanted them to die. What could they do to me? I'm already dying." The man wheezed horribly. A coughing fit shook his body.

The candle began to gutter and Turner returned to the shelf for another. "I can take you back to the hospital," he said as he sat back down.

"There's no need. They can't do anything for me. I have a home-care nurse in once a day. He's sufficient."

Candle lit and placed carefully next to the first, lightning and thunder roaring without, Gravelstone talked on.

"I was among the inner circle. A few months ago I became too ill to continue attending meetings. A friend told me they'd chosen violence. I knew I could die in peace. When the Reverend Mucklewrath's daughter died, I knew they'd started. I felt great joy when I listened to the news. Glad and warmed in my heart in a way I hadn't felt since I said my first mass."

He sighed deeply and stopped. He closed his eyes and for a moment Turner thought he might die at that instant, but the old eyes resumed their implacable gaze, and the story continued. "I helped plan some of the early attacks, the tamer ones, like the pictures of the bishop. I loved the look on his face in the light of the camera flash."

"Why did Wilmer die?" Turner asked softly. He had to lean even closer to hear the reply.

"Because I'm a fool. After all these years, my greatest fault is still being a fool." He began to cry, quietly at first and then almost uncontrollably.

Turner reached over and pulled him close and held him tight. Gravelstone's arms barely had the strength to clutch him back.

168

When the sobs eased and Gravelstone lay back, Turner brought him toilet paper from the bathroom so the old man could blow his nose and wipe his tears.

Finally the old man continued, "I'm a fool, because after all these years, shunned and hated by the Catholic church, I still needed to confess. I never killed anyone, but I had a hand in planning the killings others did and will do, and in organizing the harm they have done and still hope to do, and I needed to confess. I had sinned and I knew it. I had to tell. I tried to confess to a real priest in a real church. That clerical jerk in the hospital might as well be a fixture on a holy card for all he's good for. I managed it once on my own, to get to a church. I sat in the confessional and found, after thirty years, I couldn't whisper secrets in some medieval hiding hole.

"So I told Wilmer. The only man who talked to me and cared for me in thirty years, who wasn't concerned about my past. He knew how to listen. Amazingly enough, the dear old soul had morals. How was I to know?"

Tears coursed down his cheeks. "I told him and I killed him. He said he would go to other members of the organization and try to stop them. I picked the wrong person to tell. Poor Wilmer believed in laws and rules and the inevitability of time making all things right. He's a bigger fool than I am. He promised not to reveal his source and I was too ill to stop him. They didn't know I knew him. Only that cute young thing in the hospital knew, and what did he care? They wouldn't think to ask an innocent straight boy."

With growing unease Turner thought: At least one person asked.

Gravelstone continued, "How did you know to talk to him?"

"Persistence and luck," Turner said, then asked, "Why were my children threatened?"

"I wasn't around then. Had to be sheer overzealous amateurism. I could have told them to leave the cops alone. Once they started, they probably couldn't stop."

"Who is 'they'?" Turner asked.

"Slowly, young man. I'll tell you some, but not all. I signed

169

Wilmer's death warrant. I will avenge that. He threatened them, and with our initial attacks going so successfully his threats enraged the entire council and our leader. He alone ordered Wilmer killed, I'm sure of it. My best and only friend dead for my mistake. The closest thing I've had to a lover in my whole life. I will hate him forever for that."

Turner wasn't sure which "him" Gravelstone referred to. He began to ask but the old man held up a hand.

"I killed him by confessing."

Turner said, "I'll find you a priest who you can talk to, confess to. I promise you that."

Gravelstone clutched at Turner's hand with an intensity that surprised the policeman. "God bless you for that, but you must do something else. You must catch Wilmer's killer and be sure he is punished. You must avenge his murder."

The old man let go his grip and sank back into his pillows. "I need to rest," he said.

Again Turner had to lean close to hear the next words. "I'm sorry about your children. If I'd known you, it would be different. Go, my son. The ultimate planner who held us together no matter what, who ordered Wilmer's death—go, get him. Dr. George Manfred is not a very nice man after all."

Disbelief and fear raced to master Turner's emotions. A thousand more questions rushed through his mind at this confirmation of his worst fears, but the old man, too stubborn or too ill, would answer no more. Turner knew George Manfred planned to visit his son that evening. Might already have done so, might have hurt his boy. Manfred would have no problem with a security guard. Paul couldn't afford to take the chance anything the old man said was a lie.

As quickly as possible, he helped the old man get comfortable. Promising once again to bring or send a priest, he left.

Once outside he raced down the stairs and flew toward the car. The crashing rain resoaked him instantly. Thunder boomed and lightning slammed above him.

He ignored it all.

The car started with a roar. He reversed out of the parking

space, shoved the car into drive, and floored it. The tires spun and swerved on the wet pavement. The rear end fishtailed. He paused a second to let the tires catch, then hit the accelerator again.

On the car radio he called the station and got Charlie Grimwald. He ordered, "Get somebody to Mrs. Talucci and Brian now, and alert the hospital." He explained the need.

Charlie said okay and told him the lieutenant wanted to talk to him. Turner heard the lieutenant say they were trying to send cars to the hospital, but with the rain itself and all the subsequent accidents, it would be difficult.

The old man's confession left too many things unexplained. Turner wanted answers and would get them, but first he had to make sure his boys were safe. He raced back to I-57, spraying jets of water from his tires' wake. His hope of rushing through town by expressway died after 103rd Street. At that point he ran into a completely stopped line of cars. The rotating light on the top of his vehicle made no dent in the movement ahead. Undoubtedly underpasses on the Dan Ryan had flooded. He didn't hesitate. He pulled onto the shoulder and rode it to the Halsted Street exit. Even with his siren bellowing and lights flashing, he made torturously slow progress up the city streets. His radio contact told him the hospital reported all normal; Brian was at Mrs. Talucci's, with a cop in the house. Still his fear increased with every flooded intersection he had to skirt. The chaos of the downpour mixed with the height of rush hour caused him endless minutes of mind-numbing anxiety. At each delay he became more aware of the horror and helplessness Mucklewrath must have felt when he saw his daughter murdered.

The pouring rain kept on. The flashing red light and the screaming siren barely penetrated the rain thundering on the roof. Still Halsted Street proved faithful all the way to Lake Street. Here the flooded intersection forced him to halt.

He slammed his hand on the steering wheel, then spun it far to the right. The car swerved up Lake Street toward the Loop. His speed caused him to send up geysers from the standing water on the street. As long as the car didn't stall, he didn't care.

Up Orleans, he jogged over to Clybourn and took it back to Halsted. He snaked around a three-car accident at the corner of North and Halsted and continued on.

Turner roared up to the hospital. He didn't feel the rain as he jumped from the car and raced inside.

In the hall he found everything very quiet. He sped past the night nurse station, hearing calls behind him.

He punched the elevator button, but in almost the same instant saw the sign for the stairs. He took them two at a time, oblivious to his labored breathing. He flung open the door on the fourth floor. Again total quiet. Nurses to the left of him called his name. He turned to the right. No security guard.

He rushed to Jeff's room. His son slept peacefully. George Manfred stood over the boy, the only light in the room outlining his figure from behind, casting a dark shadow over the boy.

"You motherfucking son of a bitch. Get away from my son." Turner aimed his gun at Manfred's head.

George turned his soft brown eyes on him and looked at him in alarm. "What's wrong, Paul?" he asked.

The door of the room banged open. Several of the staff walked in. The gun stopped them. Paul held up his star in his left hand so the people who entered could see it, while he kept his gun in his right hand trained on the doctor.

"How'd this bastard get in here?" Turner demanded. A large man in a security-guard uniform, seemingly in charge, said, "They told us to be careful of danger. Dr. Manfred isn't dangerous. He was here, so I went to get a cup of coffee."

"You stupid shit. The rest of the police will be here in a minute," he said. "Until they get here make sure no one else is around who isn't supposed to be. Put a guard on this door so no one gets in. For now, all of you, out!"

Seeing the gun and recognizing his forceful commands, the hospital staff retreated.

Turner said to Manfred, "Over by the other bed. Keep your hands where I can see them."

172

"Paul?" Manfred said.

"Just keep moving."

Manfred moved behind the empty bed on the far side of the room.

Without taking his eyes from Manfred, Turner reached down and felt Jeff's face and hair. The boy stirred, but slept on, oblivious as usual to all but the most vigorous attempts to wake him.

"He's fine," Manfred said.

"I've been to talk to Gravelstone," Turner began. "He explained a lot. I want the rest of the truth from you."

"What did he say?"

Turner recounted all that Gravelstone told him, finishing with, "The kid at the hospital told me you asked who Wilmer knew."

"Paul"—George spoke softly—"I know you're worried about your son. I'm sorry for that. I didn't kill anybody. Nobody in any group I'm in charge of killed anybody. We haven't done any violence at all."

"What about what Gravelstone said? All the plans?"

"In managing groups I've found it easier to let the radicals rant and rave, so they get it out of their system. They get bored, or leave. Mostly they want to be heard and paid attention to. Few really want to take the responsibility of doing something themselves. They could on their own. What do they need a group for? Only two or three people ever wanted to do violence in the first place. Two meetings after Gravelstone became too ill to attend, we decided on total nonviolence."

Turner's mind wavered. Manfred sounded so reasonable and calm.

"We did plan the diarrhea attack, the fake whorehouse story, the naked pictures of the bishop, and the author's book, but that's all. Maybe a friend told Gravelstone what he wanted to hear. If the old man was dying, what difference would it make?"

"How come the same message got left at the murder?" Turner asked.

"We planned to leave the same message each time. Paul, be

reasonable. We couldn't know the murderers would leave the same message. We had nothing to do with the violent acts."

"Burning the author's book isn't exactly nonviolent."

"No organization is perfect. They were supposed to steal every other page. We figured it'd drive Bennet nuts."

"What about Wilmer?"

"What about him?"

Turner reminded him what Gravelstone had said about Wilmer talking to them.

"Paul, he never talked to anybody. Certainly not to me. Maybe he would have if he'd had the chance. I haven't seen him in weeks."

"I'm still not convinced about this 'Sorry now' shit. That's a hell of a coincidence."

"We saw the words in the *Tribune*, connected with the legislator's house burning in Kankakee. An unfortunate decision in retrospect—but you've got to remember, we didn't plan it in conjunction with these tragedies. We didn't know the Mucklewrath murderers used those words. The police never released that information. I know it looks awful, but I repeat, we haven't done any violence at all."

Turner held the gun steady, wondered where his backup was. He glanced at his watch: seven thirty. Probably stuck in the rain and paralyzed traffic of an exhausted rush hour. "How can I believe you?" Turner asked.

They stared at each other in silence.

A commotion in the hall caused them both to turn. Paul swung his gun toward the door. The door banged open. Ian entered, a hospital orderly draped around his waist. The white-clad attendant shouted for him to stop. Ian ignored him.

Paul sorted things out. Minutes later Ian sat next to Jeff, across from Paul. "Manfred didn't kill anybody. He didn't plan to, either."

"Explain," Paul ordered.

Ian told him that he'd gotten the truth out of Gill Garret late that afternoon. As Paul listened to the story, he realized it matched Manfred's. Ian said, "I believe them. They may have done stuff that was slightly out of the ordinary, and mildly illegal, and I was wrong about them, but they didn't kill anybody."

Paul respected and trusted Ian more than anyone he knew. He said, "You believe them?"

"Yes," Ian said.

"Double fuck," Paul said. He'd long since lowered the gun. Not sure what to do or say, he sat on Jeff's bed. He looked at Manfred. "Sorry," he mumbled.

The doctor said, "You were worried about your kids."

An uncomfortable silence followed. Finally Manfred excused himself and left.

Paul checked Jeff, who still slept peacefully. In the hallway a guard stood watch.

Outside the rain had stopped. Standing next to his car Turner said, "I feel like shit for what I said to Manfred."

Ian said, "We all make mistakes. You had reason to be afraid. Don't kick yourself. Maybe things will work out between you two."

"Maybe." Turner sounded unconvinced.

After a few moments' silence Ian said, "I feel somewhat akin to a fool. I screwed up. There was never any conspiracy."

"Should I say I warned you?"

"Please don't. I'll only get more depressed. Gill only told me now because he knew if I went any further with my theories, and if I ever found out he knew the truth, I'd never forgive him. We grew up together. We've been friends since first grade. Fortunately for me, he thought friendship was more important than principle."

The air felt twenty degrees cooler. Occasional drops of water trickled off the leaves of the trees down to black pools of standing water.

"I have more news," Ian said sheepishly.

Turner waited.

"I had a little chat with Rusty this afternoon. It seemed odd to me that rumor about as prominent a person as Donald Muck-lewrath wouldn't be more current in the community. Certainly

I should have heard something. There's always rumors about famous actors, actresses, sports heroes, major public personalities, but I hadn't heard a thing about Mucklewrath. I came here from Rusty's. I thought you might be here to see Jeff. I wasn't able to get you on the phone."

"So what did the kid say?"

"I brought him a picture of Donald Mucklewrath. The man was at the party Rusty attended, but Donald wasn't the guy who propositioned Rusty. The reverend's picture is plastered over everything, but not his kid's. Who would really know? When Rusty saw the picture, he had no idea who it was."

Turner summed up. "Donald isn't gay. Rusty in his ignorance and eagerness screwed up."

"Along with a buddy who wasn't too bright, at the same party." Ian sighed. "This was a major fuckup. No Johnny, Oprah, Phil, Sally, or Joan." He uttered a soft moan. "There's more."

"You know who killed Mucklewrath's daughter?"

"No, but the fire is Kankakee? The legislator? Her opponent was on the news at four accusing her of setting it herself for the insurance money. Claimed he had proof. Said the 'Sorry now' painted on the driveway was her attempt to convince people it was a conspiracy led by her enemies."

Turner comforted his friend as best he could and got ready to leave. He opened his car door and said, "I'm tired. I want to get home."

When he got there, the house was empty. He strolled over to Mrs. Talucci's, noting the cop car out front. He entered and the door slammed behind him. He stared down the muzzle of a police .38. Beyond it was Donald Mucklewrath.

Donald led him into the living room. Mrs. Talucci sat in her rocker, glaring viciously at the reverend's son. From his place in the middle of the couch, Brian eyed his dad mutely out of one eye. The other was bruised, blackened, and so puffed it was nearly closed. A red welt trailed down the right side of his face.

"I tried to get his gun, dad."

Paul started to go to him.

"No, you don't, faggot." Donald ordered Turner to throw his gun on the floor, then motioned him to a chair on the far side of the room.

"How'd you get in here?" Turner asked.

Donald grinned, pleased with himself. "Through the back door. I tiptoed through the rain drops. All the goddamn nosy neighbors weren't looking out tonight."

"What do you want, Donald?" Turner asked.

"I'm going to shut all of you up permanently. I was only going to hurt your kid, but this goddamn busybody showed up and stuck her two cents in. Now I've got to kill you all."

To keep his eye on Paul and Brian, Donald moved closer to Mrs. Talucci. Turner hoped she didn't try anything foolish.

"I'll figure some way to stick this to the gay conspiracy. Enough saps in the world believe that shit to make it work."

"There's no gay conspiracy, or not much of one," Turner said. To stall for time he told Donald what he'd learned that night.

"That's all it was?" Donald laughed. "They're going to have to learn to be more vicious, if they want to succeed. Violence works."

"Why did you kill your sister?" Turner asked.

Donald laughed again.

From the sound of it Turner guessed the reverend's son was near the edge of a breakdown.

Donald waved the gun in the air. "I'm over thirty years old and I'm a security guard. My father makes millions, owns corporations and a university, and I'm a goddamn flunky, a nothing. They like to keep me out of the way, and now they're going to promote my goddamn stepsister to a prominent place in the campaign. They talked about making her a spokesperson, of her taking over parts of the operation when she graduated from college."

He walked over to Brian and held the gun an inch from his head. Paul and Mrs. Talucci were halfway out of their seats, but Donald swung the gun on them. "Stay there," he ordered. They subsided. He returned the gun to Brian's temple. "You got a nice kid here. How'd that happen, since you're a faggot? Did you know that, kid? That your dad screws guys?"

"Fuck you," Brian said.

That got him a smash across the other cheek that sent him sprawling. Brian didn't cry out. Moments later he sat up.

Donald returned to his original position nearer to Mrs. Talucci. He said, "I'm a nothing and going nowhere, but I knew she wasn't going to replace me. I found two of the guys I recruited to the reverend's service. I knew I could trust them. I saw my chance that morning. We gave it a try. No witnesses, or so we thought. That goddamn bum saw us. He slept in Lincoln Park that night, was walking across the pedestrian bridge near North Avenue, and saw us. He came to Soldier Field that night and got close to me somehow. He said he had information for me. He claimed he'd tell my father if I didn't confess. Said he tried to talk to you, but you turned him down. I knew he had to die. Knew I had to check out his buddies, see if he told them anything. It wasn't hard really. He was a drunk and a fool, and now"—he pointed the gun at Turner—"you have to die."

Brian lurched forward. Mucklewrath swung the gun toward him and fired. The shot never came close because Mrs. Talucci flew out of her chair the instant Mucklewrath turned toward Brian. She threw her hundred and ten pounds into a blow against the arm with the gun. The shot smashed into the ceiling. Turner moved right behind Mrs. Talucci, tackling Donald. The gun flew and Brian picked it up.

Hours later, with Donald safely arrested, Mrs. Talucci insisted they take her cure for shattered nerves. They ate ice cream and chocolate cake at her kitchen table. Brian had difficulty eating with an ice pack held to his face. Manfully he devoured three slices.

At home Paul examined his son's face in the upstairs bathroom. "Going to be a hell of an ugly face for a while," Paul said.

178

"The girls will think I'm real tough," Brian said.

"I'm glad you're all right," Paul said. He put his arm on his son's shoulder for their usual show of affection, suddenly found himself hugged fiercely. He returned his son's embrace.